I just *knew* that red balloon was going to deliver my letter to Grandma in heaven! Right after I wrote it, Grandma sent Mary to be my guardian angel—and my new mommy. I love Mary, and Daddy really likes her, too. He even kisses her…a lot! Now all Daddy has to do is marry Mary and plant some baby seeds in her tummy, and pretty soon I'll have a little brother or sister, like I've always wanted. I just wish I knew why Mary looks so sad whenever I talk about that….

Annie Taylor, Age Six

Dear Reader,

If you take a look at the back covers of our two books this month, you'll notice that each one features a multiple-choice question. I don't know about you, but taking tests was not exactly my favorite thing to do back when I was in school. (I don't think we'll discuss just how long ago that was!) However, I took both these quizzes and had no trouble at all coming up with the right answers, and I don't think you will, either.

Carla Cassidy's *Pop Goes the Question* is very aptly titled, because it's inside a helium balloon that Mary Wellington finds the note that's going to change her entire future. What I'd like to know is this, however: How come the only notes *I* ever find are discarded shopping lists? Of course, I've never been whisked away by a just-jilted groom, either, though that's exactly what happens to the heroine of Christie Ridgway's *Follow That Groom!* I think I'm going to have to start taking my life cues from these books!

Anyway, read and enjoy them, and then come back next month for two more terrific novels about meeting, dating—and marrying—Mr. Right.

Yours (truly),

Leslie J. Wainger
Senior Editor and Editorial Coordinator

Please address questions and book requests to:
Silhouette Reader Service
U.S.: 3010 Walden Ave., P.O. Box 1325, Buffalo, NY 14269
Canadian: P.O. Box 609, Fort Erie, Ont. L2A 5X3

CARLA CASSIDY

Pop Goes the Question

Published by Silhouette Books
America's Publisher of Contemporary Romance

This book is dedicated to my editor,
Karen Taylor Richman,
for her patience and encouragement.
Thanks, Karen, for teaching me how
to reach, for listening to my fears
and helping me achieve my dreams.

 SILHOUETTE BOOKS

ISBN 0-373-52037-9

POP GOES THE QUESTION

Printed in U.S.A.

About the author

I was going to be a star. At least, that's what I thought when, at the age of nineteen, I packed my bags, left my Midwestern town and headed for New York City. For a year I toured the East Coast in a band. Then fate intervened…I met a man. Not just any man, but the one who made me forget about dreams of stardom and instead made me dream of home and family.

Professional cheerleader for a national football team, actress, singer and dancer, I've had more than my share of exciting challenges. However, by far the most wonderful has been keeping the fires alive in my twenty-year marriage and writing stories that share my happiness and touch readers' emotions.

I traded my dreams of stardom, but I managed to get one heck of a leading man.

Books by Carla Cassidy

Silhouette Yours Truly

Pop Goes the Question

Silhouette Romance

Patchwork Family #818
Whatever Alex Wants... #856
Fire and Spice #884
Homespun Hearts #905
Golden Girl #924
Something New #942
Pixie Dust #958
The Littlest Matchmaker #978
The Marriage Scheme #996
Anything for Danny #1048
Deputy Daddy #1141
Mom in the Making #1147
An Impromptu Proposal #1152
Daddy on the Run #1158

Silhouette Desire

A Fleeting Moment #784
Under the Boardwalk #882

Silhouette Shadows

Swamp Secrets #4
Heart of the Beast #11
Silent Screams #25
Mystery Child #61

* The Baker Brood

Silhouette Intimate Moments

One of the Good Guys #531
Try To Remember #560
Fugitive Father #604

Silhouette Books

Silhouette Shadows
  Short Stories 1993
  "Devil and the Deep Blue Sea"

The Loop

Getting it Right: Jessica

1

"Are you sure Grandma will get my letter?" Five-year-old Annie looked up at her father for assurance. The wind in the cemetery whipped her pale blond ringlets around her face, momentarily obscuring her vivid blue eyes.

Jonathon Taylor held the string of the red helium balloon tightly in one hand as he bent down on his haunches to face his daughter. He gently swiped a strand of her fine hair away from her eyes, his heart aching with both her grief and his own. "Look, right here on the balloon we've written everything necessary to make certain she gets it. To Grandma Taylor. Address, Heaven."

Annie nodded solemnly. "Can I say a prayer before we let it go?"

Jonathon nodded and stood back up, watching as his daughter approached the gravestone marked: Regina Taylor. Beloved Wife, Mother and Grandmother.

It was amazing, really, the lengths a grown, rational man would go to just to appease the aching heart of a little girl. Though his mother, God rest her loving soul, might have argued that he was neither completely grown, nor fully rational.

However, since his mother's death a month ago, he certainly was the single parent to a little girl who didn't understand death any more than she understood the workings of a twin-engine Cessna.

He stared at his daughter as she knelt at the graveside, whispering fervently into clasped hands. As always, whenever he gazed at Annie, his heart filled up, expanded to enormous proportions in his chest. She was his heart, what kept him grounded, what made him whole, and he hoped releasing a balloon to heaven would help ease her sadness over the loss of her grandmother.

Now that the shock of the death of his mother was beginning to wear off and neighbors and friends had slowly withdrawn the flurry of emotional support that always accompanied death, Jonathon had to admit he was overwhelmed by the awesome responsibility left to him.

For the past five years, Jonathon's mother had been his rock, playing the maternal role in Annie's life since Annie's mother had walked out on them three months after Annie's birth.

Now everything had changed. Last week he'd abandoned his flying career for a permanent teaching job at the community college, and starting now he would be the sole caretaker for his little girl.

It was a daunting thought. He'd been dependent on his mother to provide the feminine, softer touches that a little girl needed.

His sister constantly told him what he needed was a wife, but Jonathon had almost given up on finding a woman who would be a good wife to him and a loving mother to Annie. He was beginning to believe no such woman existed.

Annie stood up and walked back over to him, her face far too sober for a little girl. "Okay, I'm ready now."

He nodded and carefully handed her the string to the balloon. She stared at it for a long moment, then raised her arm straight up toward the sky. She released the balloon.

Together they watched as it rose steadily upward, then dipped and swayed with the currents of the cool spring wind. It danced against the backdrop of the perfect spring blue sky, came teasingly close to the limbs of a tree, then shot straight up. They watched until the red balloon had disappeared from sight, then Annie turned and held out her hand for his. "Is Grandma in the same heaven with Mommy?"

Jonathon nodded, although he had serious doubts that his ex-wife had ever made it to heaven after she'd been killed in a tragic car accident three years ago. However, if by some miracle Katherine had gone to heaven, she'd better find an angel wing to hide behind if she ran into Jonathon's mother.

Regina Taylor had had little love in her heart for the woman who'd married Jonathon, given birth to Annie, then walked out because she'd decided she didn't want to be married or be a mother.

"I'm hungry. When are we gonna eat supper?"

Jonathon stared at his daughter blankly. Supper? Was it that late? Hadn't they just had lunch at Annie's favorite drive-through? He looked at his wristwatch and gasped. Lunch had been hours ago.

"You promised pizza, Daddy."

Damn, he'd forgotten all about the promise of pizza for supper. "Honey, don't you remember? Tonight is the night we were going to have dinner with Sonia in a fancy restaurant so you two can meet and get to know each other."

Annie frowned. "Can't we get to know each other in a pizza place?"

Jonathon hesitated. He'd had three dates with the gorgeous flight attendant, Sonia Wakefield, and he didn't think she was exactly the pizza parlor type. But he'd made a promise to Annie, and she was his number one priority.

"I think you could get to know each other just fine in a pizza place," he agreed.

Annie clapped her hands and gave him a sweet smile that shot straight through to his heart. "I love you, Daddy."

He grabbed her up in his arms and headed for the car. "I love you, too, Annie." As she wrapped her arms around his neck and he smelled the childish scent of strawberry bubble bath and sunshine, all his previous worries about raising his daughter all by himself melted away. He had a feeling he and Annie were going to be just fine.

Mary Wellington had been in a bad mood for the past two months, every since her latest Mr. Right had transformed into Mr. Wrong. As always when she first opened her eyes in the morning, she automatically rolled over to stare at the pillow next to her own. Pristine, untouched, no depression from the head of a significant other. What a rotten, depressing way to start a new day.

She rolled over on her back and slapped the quilt with the back of her hand. Wasted. She had wasted nearly a year of her life in a relationship with a dark-haired, blue-eyed pseudo cowboy who'd left her last month.

He'd left behind a six-pack of beer in her refrigerator, spur marks on her wooden floors and a vicious cat named Cowpoke whose sole purpose for living was to make her life miserable. How on earth could she have ever thought herself seriously in love with a man who referred to lovemaking as "riding the range?" And now she was alone on the range.

"Ugh!" She rolled out of bed and headed for the shower, hoping to wash thoughts of the dysfunctional relationship down the drain.

Minutes later, with one towel wrapped sarong-style around her body and another turban-style around her head, she walked back into her bedroom.

"Cowpoke!" she shrieked at the large tomcat who was alternately sharpening his claws and eating her panty hose.

"Scat," she screeched, moaning as she held up the ruined hose ... her last pair. At times she wondered if Cowpoke hadn't been a gift of retribution, payment for all those times she'd secretly applauded when an Indian had shot a cowboy in an old western movie.

She threw the stockings in the trash, then realized if she didn't hurry she'd be late for work. She dressed in a cotton blouse and a long skirt that hid the fact that she was sans hose, then raced a brush through her wet brown hair. Hopefully it would dry before she got to work. Thank goodness she'd been blessed with naturally curly hair and didn't have to bother with curling irons or hot rollers.

Dr. Burwell would be upset if she was late again. One of these days she would learn the lesson of the dangers of snooze buttons on her alarm clock. She'd punched it four times this morning...three times too many.

With a final scowl at Cowpoke, who lounged in the middle of her bed looking infinitely superior, Mary grabbed her purse and the lunch she'd made the night before, and left the apartment.

As she drove the three miles to the doctor's office where she worked as a receptionist, she tried to keep her mind firmly schooled against ruminating on her disastrous love life.

She had an irritating habit of walking into a social event and attracting the most dysfunctional, emotionally needy male in the room. She was beginning to believe that was her mission in life, to heal these men so they could move on to wonderfully successful relationships with other women.

She gunned her car to pass a slower one, earning a honk and a prominent flip of a finger from the driver who was on a car phone. He glared at her as if she'd personally ruined his day. She probably broke his cellular connection. Oh, good, she thought, knowing with her luck she would find herself on a blind date with him next week and he would remember the drab brunette who'd ruined his important business call.

As she pulled into the parking lot of the medical building, her attention was instantly captured by a bright red balloon floating lazily in the early morning sunshine. She parked and got out of her car, her gaze still riveted on the balloon. It looked cheerfully out of place as it dipped and bowed, coming closer and closer to the ground.

For some indefinable reason, she wanted it. The sight of it made her remember childhood birthday parties and simpler times when happiness wasn't so damned elusive. She raced after it, jumping up to capture the string in her hand. She missed, her long skirt wrapped around her legs, and she nearly fell.

She looked around, wondering if anyone was watching her antics. Trying again, she hiked up her skirt in one hand and jumped once more, laughing with abandon as the balloon eluded her, then danced teasingly close. Gasping for breath, she tried once more, this time successfully catching the string.

She held it against her chest for a moment, like a child with a cherished possession. Suddenly the morning irritations faded away. It was a beautiful spring morning and she had caught a balloon. She laughed aloud, realizing she must look silly. A twenty-nine-year-old woman clutching a balloon in the middle of a parking lot, she could almost hear her mother's voice. ''Now, that certainly is not the kind of behavior that will attract the right kind of man, Mary." Ah, and Patricia Wilshire knew all about the right kind of man for her daughter... unfortunately, as far as Mary was concerned, the right kind of men were boring. Besides, there weren't too many men who wanted a woman who couldn't give them children. Unfortunately, Mary would never conceive a baby, never experience the joy of childbirth.

Shoving these painful thoughts out of her mind, she looked at her watch and groaned. She was now officially ten minutes late. She ran toward the office door and flung it open. Just as she sank into her seat at her desk, Dr. Burwell walked in.

"Morning, Mary," he said.

"Good morning, Dr. Burwell," she replied, easing the balloon from her lap to the floor beneath her desk where it was hidden from the old doctor's view.

"I'll be in my office."

She nodded and watched as he disappeared down the long hallway. She didn't move until she heard the familiar click of his office door closing, then she pulled the balloon back into her lap. One side of it had marker writing, and she was aware that there was something inside. She could feel it bouncing around.

"Hey, what have you got there?"

Mary started at the female voice behind her. She turned around to see Lucinda Walker, the office nurse and one of her best friends.

"It was drifting around in the parking lot," Mary explained.

"Somebody's written on it. What does it say?" Lucinda moved closer.

Mary held it up toward the light. "It says, 'To Grandma Taylor. Address, Heaven.'"

"Oh, isn't that cute?"

Mary nodded. "There's something inside. Hand me those scissors."

"You'd better hope it doesn't explode and give Doc a heart attack," Lucinda said with a giggle.

"Maybe I'd better wait." Mary hesitated. Doc Burwell had no sense of humor whatsoever.

"Oh, go ahead," Lucinda urged. "Goodness knows you need some excitement to perk up your boring life."

Mary looked at Lucinda wryly. "My boring life?"

Lucinda laughed. "You've got to admit, Mary, now that Wild Bill Hickok has ridden off into the sunset, your social life stinks."

"There's nothing wrong with my social life," Mary said defensively, jabbing the balloon with more force than she intended. Thankfully, it didn't explode, but rather hissed its helium mournfully into the air.

"It is a note," Lucinda exclaimed as Mary extricated a folded sheet of paper.

At that moment the front door to the office opened and both Lucinda and Mary jumped. Mary shoved the note into her top desk drawer and the remnants of the balloon hit the trash can. Lucinda grabbed a file folder and headed for the doctor's office.

The morning passed in a flurry of activity. A virus was making the rounds, and there was a steady stream of small patients with sore throats, fevers and hacking coughs. Mary was kept busy pulling patient folders, answering the telephone and dispensing tissues.

It had been Mary's mother who'd encouraged her to become a medical receptionist. "Think of all the doctors you'll meet," her mother had said. "You'd make a wonderful doctor's wife."

Patricia Wilshire should know. After Mary's father had died, Patricia married Barry Wilshire, a retired doctor. What Patricia hadn't foreseen was her daughter getting a job working for a very old, very married pediatrician, whose patients were all under the age of thirteen. Definitely not a terrific way to find good marriage material.

Still, Mary loved her job and had a special affinity for each and every child who came into the office. Knowing she would never have a family of her own, she found it easy to give her heart to each and every little patient.

It was noon before Mary remembered the note from the balloon. She was alone in the office, eating her sack lunch at her desk. Dr. Burwell always went home for his midday meal, and Lucinda had a lunch date with a man she'd met the night before in a singles bar.

Mary finished her soggy tuna sandwich, then opened her desk drawer and removed the folded piece of paper. The letter had been written by a young child. The letters were in red crayon and irregular in size.

Dear Grandma Taylor,
I miss you. Daddy says you are in heaven. I hope you are happy there, but I wish you were still here to take care of me. In two weeks Daddy is going to give me a big sixth birthday party. It won't be the same without you here. Does it hurt to be dead? Oh, Grandma, I worry about you. If you could just let me know that you're okay, then I'd feel so much better.

If you're really up in Heaven, maybe you could talk to somebody about getting me a little sister or a brother. I think that would be very nice. I'd be a good big sister. But Daddy says he needs a wife first, and he's not doing a very good job finding one. Maybe you could talk to somebody up there about helping him out. I love you, Grandma.

Your granddaughter,
Annie

Mary held the note for a long moment. It was obvious an adult had helped the child write the letter, but the emotion between the simply written lines caused Mary's heart to expand in sympathy. The note was dated three days earlier, and beneath Annie's signature she had written her address, which was in a suburb of Kansas City, some twenty miles away.

She reread the note. Someplace in the northern part of Kansas City was a little girl who desperately missed her grandmother and who was going to have a birthday party.

A lump rose in Mary's throat as she thought of her own grandmother. God, she hadn't thought about her in years. Mary's grandmother had died when Mary was ten, but Mary could still remember the grief, the sudden aching emptiness, and the fear that death had brought.

She picked up the note again. "Poor little girl," she whispered, then, realizing the good doctor would be back any moment, she put the note back into her drawer and got busy pulling the patient files for the afternoon.

It was as she was leaving the office at the end of the day that she thought of the note again. An idea had been playing in the back of her mind all afternoon. Instead of heading directly for her car, her footsteps took her toward the gift shop in the next block.

Once inside the little store, she wandered around, looking for the perfect birthday gift for a special little girl who missed her grandmother. As she saw the dolls, the wooden blocks, all the things especially for children, the grief that was never far from the surface surged inside her.

She'd been devastated when at the age of twenty-five she'd had to have a hysterectomy due to a severe case of endometriosis. She would never know the joy of pregnancy, the miracle of bearing a child of her own. She would never carry a seed of love inside her, would never have a child who looked like both herself and her husband. Her boyfriend at the time had soon broken off with her, sheepishly telling her that someday he wanted children...not adopted ones, but his own.

Most of the time she dealt very well with the fact she wouldn't be able to have kids, but there were still odd moments when she mourned for what would never be, what could never be.

The only constant lingering effect was on her love life. The fact that she couldn't have children made her less acceptable as wife material. She supposed the logical thing for her to do was to find a man who hated children and marry him. Unfortunately, she knew she could never love a man who hated children.

Shoving this depressing subject out of her mind, she concentrated on the charming jewelry, the one-of-a-kind handmade crafts and toys. In a bushel basket of cloth dolls she found exactly what she wanted—an angel doll complete with silvery wings and a silver-and-white gown. A perfect gift from a grandmother in heaven. She was certain Annie would love it. "Can you wrap this and send it from here?" she asked the cashier.

"Of course," the woman replied. "Would you like to include a card or a note?"

"A note," Mary agreed, smiling her thanks as the woman handed her a piece of pale lavender stationery with a pastel floral design. Frowning in thought, Mary quickly wrote a note to Annie, then gave it and the address to the shopkeeper, who promised to have it delivered the day of the little girl's birthday.

As Mary left the store she felt curiously light-hearted. It didn't matter that she was going home to a frozen diet dinner, television and an attack cat with a bad attitude. Hopefully she'd just done something that would make a little girl very happy. Not a bad way to end a day.

"You didn't mention your daughter is so young," Sonia said softly, one of her pale blond eyebrows arched upward.

Jonathon answered her with a raised eyebrow of his own. On their three previous dates, he knew he'd told Sonia all about Annie, and he suddenly realized that whenever he'd talked about his daughter, Sonia had apparently tuned him out. Definitely not a good sign.

"I'm gonna be six next week," Annie exclaimed.

"How nice," Sonia said, not taking her eyes off Jonathon. She reached out to lightly caress the upper sleeve of his shirt. "For some reason, I just thought she was much older, more independent."

Jonathon smiled faintly. He must have been crazy to think that a woman like Sonia had a place in his and Annie's life. He had a feeling Sonia didn't have a maternal bone in her body.

"I'm old for my age," Annie proclaimed. "Aren't I, Daddy?"

"Definitely," Jonathon agreed with a grin. "There are times I'd swear that you were almost seven."

Sonia's hot pink fingernails scratched lightly on his skin, igniting the beginning flame of desire as she flirtatiously fluttered her eyelids. Oh, the woman had eyes that promised wonderful sins of the flesh.

She raised her wineglass to her pouty full lips. She took a sip, then ran her tongue along the edge of the glass. Jonathon could easily imagine those full red lips nipping at his own...moving down the length of his body to lick...

"Perhaps little Annie will go to bed early this evening?" Sonia said softly. "That way we could have some quality time alone."

"Daddy?"

Jonathon tore his gaze from Sonia and turned to his daughter, who had a piece of mozzarella cheese dangling off her chin.

"How come she keeps doing this?" Annie batted her eyelashes in a surprisingly good parody of Sonia, then carefully licked around the edge of her soda glass, causing a sloppy mixture of sauce and cheese to coat the rim of the glass.

Jonathon stared speechlessly at his daughter as Sonia gasped indignantly. When he looked back at his date, the promise he'd seen earlier in her eyes was gone and the full, pouty lips were pressed into a taut, narrow line.

He suddenly laughed, unable to contain his mirth. He swallowed hard and smiled sheepishly at Sonia, who didn't smile back. He looked at his daughter, who grinned happily, a piece of mushroom decorating the end of her nose like a mutant freckle.

He turned back to his date. She suddenly didn't look the least bit appealing to him. "Actually, Sonia, I promised Annie she and I would watch the late movie tonight, so as soon as we finish eating, I'll just take you right home."

"That's certainly fine with me," Sonia answered coolly, her eyes no longer promising, but damning.

Jonathon grinned, not disappointed at all that this would be his last date with Sonia Wakefield. He winked at his daughter, who winked back, the mushroom falling from the end of her nose.

2

━━━━◄━━━━

"Mother, I told you that I didn't want you to fix me up with any more blind dates," Mary protested. She twisted the phone cord more tightly around her thumb, watching as it turned blue. "That last date you arranged was a complete fiasco."

"Roger was such a cute young man. How was I to know he was married?" Patricia exclaimed.

"And had a wife stalking him," Mary reminded her mother, then shuddered at that particular memory. "What a nightmare."

"Darling, don't look at this one as a blind date. Consider it fate. Heaven knows you aren't doing a very good job of finding a nice man for yourself," Patricia said, and Mary could easily envision her mother's self-satisfied smile. "I really think you and Herman are just perfect for each other."

Mary sighed and unwound the cord from her thumb. She found it difficult to believe that the perfect man for her was named Herman. "Oh, Mother," she said, sighing again.

"Mary, all I want you to do is just give him a chance. Herman Walsh is a wonderful doctor, and he's been divorced for several years. He's in the market for a wife and doesn't want any more children."

"What kind of a doctor is he?" Mary asked, resigned to the fact that her mother wasn't going to give up until she agreed to go out with Dr. Walsh. At least a man who didn't want more children had one positive strike on his side.

"He has a very successful practice."

A dull dread resounded in the pit of Mary's stomach. "Mother, what kind of a doctor is he?" she repeated.

"He's a podiatrist. Mary, you're almost thirty years old, you can't be as picky as you once might have been."

Mary stifled a groan. She drew in a deep breath. Okay, so the guy's name was Herman and he was a podiatrist. What was in a name, anyway? And being a foot doctor was a perfectly respectable profession. "So when is this date supposed to take place?"

"Friday night. I told him how much you loved the ballet, and he's got two tickets for *Swan Lake* at the Music Hall. He's going to pick you up at seven. Oh, and wear your hair up, it makes you look more sophisticated.''

After hanging up, the dull dread continued to course through Mary. She hated blind dates, especially the ones arranged by her mother. Mary would like to think her mother was right, that somehow this date had been arranged by fate and Dr. Herman Foot would be the man destined to be her Mr. Right.

However, she had the sinking feeling that fate was once again just laughing at her, playing tricks like a mischievous imp with a perverted sense of humor.

''You're almost thirty years old, you can't be as picky as you once might have been.'' Her mother's words echoed in her head, causing a slight ache to start right between her eyes. Thirty wasn't so old, was it? She didn't exactly have one foot on a banana peel and the other in the grave. There was still time for her to find a good man, one with whom she could share the rest of her life.

She changed into her pajamas and climbed into bed, ignoring Cowpoke's irritable meow as she invaded what the cat considered its personal space.

Perhaps she was destined to never marry, she thought. Lots of women led full, happy lives without the benefit of matrimony. However, Mary didn't want to be one of those women. She wanted a special someone in her life, somebody to share her triumphs and her failures, somebody who would inspire passion and dreams. Cowpoke crawled into the crook of her legs, tickling her skin with soft fur as a rumbling purr vibrated the bed. Yes, Mary wanted somebody special in her life, preferably somebody without fur.

By Friday night Mary felt as schizophrenic as her cat. As she dressed for her date she alternated between a terrible sense of dread and a thrill of excitement. Maybe this would finally be her Mr. Right. Perhaps he would finally be the man she'd been waiting for, the person who had filled her dreams, her handsome prince. Or maybe he would be just another warty toad.

By the time her doorbell rang, announcing the arrival of Herman Walsh, Mary was a mass of nervous energy. She'd dressed with care in a chic red dress her mother had bought her for her last birthday.

However, contrary to her mother's wishes, her light brown hair was loose and curly to her shoulders. There wasn't a sophisticated bone in Mary's body, and to put her hair up and pretend otherwise was like false advertising. If a man was going to fall in love with her, he was going to have to accept her just the way she was, with all her faults and foibles.

Taking a deep breath, she opened her door. Standing on her porch in a plaid suit and paisley tie was Dr. Herman Walsh, looking more like a stereo-typical used-car salesman than a dignified doctor.

"Mary?"

She nodded, and he grinned in obvious relief.

"Oh, wow, this is great." He looked her up and down, then grinned again. "I was afraid you'd be really ugly or something. I mean, with your mother setting up this date and all. She didn't say you were ugly or anything like that, but most mothers don't think their daughters are dogs even when they are."

My mother must secretly hate me, Mary thought as Herman rambled on about his various blind dates in the past. "Uh...shouldn't we be going?" she finally asked when the man finally stopped to draw in a deep breath.

"Oh, yeah, we'd better get going," he agreed. "We don't want to miss the overture." He waited as she locked the front door, then he took her by the elbow and led her out to his car, a sleek sports model that gleamed with polish and wax.

Mary tried desperately to like Herman. She wanted to like him. It didn't matter to her that he didn't seem to possess any fashion sense, nor did she care that he fell asleep halfway through the ballet and snored until the final curtain.

Physically, he wasn't exactly unattractive. He had nice hair and a smile that crinkled the corners of his brown eyes. It didn't matter to Mary that he had a paunch and that she suspected his gorgeous hair wasn't really his own. As her mother so often reminded her, she couldn't afford to be as picky as she'd once been.

Herman insisted they go for coffee after the performance, and while he told her bad feet jokes, Mary wondered what on earth she could have done to her mother that would make the woman think Herman was perfect for her.

The one thing Mary found fascinating about the man was a single strand of hair. Between the middle of his eyebrows, directly above his nose, it protruded out like a unicorn horn. What Mary found interesting was that it moved up and down, like a dowsing stick seeking water, when he talked. And the man could talk . . . a lot.

"Thank you, Herman. I had an interesting time," she said as he walked her back to her apartment door.

"Yeah, it was great. Maybe we could go see a movie or something next weekend?"

He looked at her so eagerly, Mary didn't have the heart to tell him no. She merely nodded. "I'm not sure what my schedule will be, so give me a call later in the week."

"Oh, I'll do that," he assured her with a toothy grin. "And you be sure and tell all your friends that Dr. Herman Walsh is the best bunion man in town."

He winked. "That's because I'm a foot doctor with sole." He laughed, his hair bounced, and Mary felt nauseous.

With a quick goodbye, she closed her door and breathed a sigh of relief. She'd never been more happy to see a date end. Poor guy. Someday Herman Walsh would find the woman of his dreams, but it wasn't going to be Mary.

She walked into her bedroom and turned on the light. Cowpoke stretched and eyed her lazily from the center of the bed. "Well, you have nothing to worry about, Cowpoke," she said as she undressed. "It doesn't look like you're going to have a new man in your life yet." She yanked her nightgown over her head, suddenly overwhelmed with a feeling of acute loneliness.

There were nights when she thought being with her pseudo cowboy would be better than being alone. At least he'd filled the apartment with noise instead of the overpowering silence that surrounded her now.

She went into the bathroom and scrubbed off her makeup, then walked back into the bedroom and shut off the light. With the soft illumination of the moon to guide her, she got into bed, displacing the cat, who meowed and spat in protest.

The moonlight shining in through her lacy curtains created lovely patterns of light on the ceiling. Mary's mother had once had an old pair of lace curtains much like the ones at Mary's window. When Mary was little, she'd played dress-up with the swatches of lace. She was never a fairy princess or a ballet dancer, like most of her friends. Instead Mary always pretended to be a bride.

Cloaked in the lace and carrying a bouquet of dandelions, Mary orchestrated many wedding ceremonies in her backyard, with stuffed animals and dolls in attendance. Funny, now that she thought about it, even in her childhood fantasies, she'd never imagined a groom.

She frowned and turned over on her side and suddenly thought of the red balloon and the note that had been addressed to a woman in heaven.

Tomorrow was Annie Taylor's sixth birthday. The note had said her father was throwing her a big birthday party. Mary hoped the store delivered her present as promised.

She smiled, thinking of the party that would take place the next day. There would be brightly colored balloons and crepe paper, party hats and favors. And there would be children ... lots and lots of children, laughing and singing songs, playing games and having fun. With a smile still lingering on her lips, Mary drifted into pleasant dreams.

"Daddy, I think Billy threw up."

Jonathon stared at his daughter, barely able to

comprehend what she'd said amid the din. Surely he'd heard her wrong. "What?" He bent closer to her.

"I think Billy threw up in the bushes." Annie pointed to the bushes that lined the back of the yard.

Jonathon skirted the kids playing on the swing set, passed three girls jumping rope, and finally made his way to where Billy stood, his freckled face stark white. "Hey, Billy, you okay?"

"I dunno, Mr. Taylor." The little red-haired boy rubbed his tummy. "I think I ate too many hot dogs. I threw up." He pointed to a nearby bush.

"You think maybe I should call your mom to come and get you?"

"No way," Billy protested. "We haven't played games or eaten ice cream and cake yet. I don't want to go home."

"Problems?"

Jonathon turned and looked at his sister gratefully. "Billy isn't feeling too hot, but he doesn't want to go home."

Rachel placed a comforting hand on the little boy's shoulder. "Billy, why don't you go sit for a few minutes on one of the lounge chairs on the porch? I'm sure as soon as those hot dogs digest a little, you'll feel better."

He nodded and took off in the direction of the porch. Jonathon grinned at his sister. "He throwed up," he said, mimicking his little girl.

Rachel laughed and linked an arm with his. "I'm not surprised. He ate seven hot dogs. I counted."

Jonathon patted her arm. "God, I'm so glad you're here to help with all this. I had no idea what I was getting myself into."

She shook her head ruefully. "I can't believe you invited the entire day-care center."

He sighed and looked around the backyard, which was filled with children. "How was I to know so many of them would come?"

Rachel laughed once again. "Honey, you throw a party and every mother in town sees it as an opportunity to get rid of their kids for a couple of hours."

Jonathon's gaze sought his daughter. "As long as Annie's having fun, then it's worth the hassle." He smiled as he spied his daughter, a golden paper crown on her head and a happy smile decorating her face.

"What you need is a wife," Rachel said as they walked back toward the porch.

"Right. I need a wife, Annie needs a mother. Unfortunately, the women I meet don't seem to have the kind of attributes it takes to be both." Jonathon sighed, as always depressed when the subject turned to marriage and family.

For the past two years he'd been desperately seeking a woman to fit his needs, one who would be a lover and companion for him, and a mother and support for Annie.

"What about that flight attendant you were seeing? I thought that was getting pretty serious."

He shook his head, thinking of the lovely Sonia. "It was getting hot... but not serious. She was incredibly attractive, but she wouldn't have been a good mother to Annie." He sighed. "I'm beginning to think there is no woman who can be good for both me and Annie."

Rachel squeezed his arm affectionately. "Actually, I have a friend...."

"Oh, no," Jonathon protested good-naturedly. "The last friend you set me up with had purple hair and was into leather and chains. Definitely too adventurous for me."

"I agree, I made a mistake with Cookie. But honestly, Jonathon, Belinda is a wonderful woman, and she loves children. In fact, she's a second-grade teacher." Rachel smiled sheepishly. "And I told her you'd pick her up at noon tomorrow for a picnic at the zoo."

"You what?" Jonathon glowered at his sister.

"Daddy, can we play some games now?" Annie tugged on his hand.

Jonathon looked down at his daughter, then back at his sister. "We'll talk about this later," he promised ominously.

Rachel merely smiled as Annie tugged him away.

Two hours later the last of the revelers left. Jonathon stood in the middle of the backyard clutching trash bags and glanced around in astonishment. It looked like a bomb had exploded. It would take him hours to pick up the clutter.

"Might as well get started," he murmured. Rachel was in the kitchen, trying to clear up the disarray in there. He suddenly wondered if the party had been worth the mess.

"Daddy?"

He turned to see Annie coming toward him. "Hi, pumpkin. Did you have fun today?"

She threw her arms around his neck and kissed his cheek. "It was the bestest birthday party in the whole wide world," she announced.

As she cuddled against him, he knew the party had been worth all the effort, all the mess—even Billy's unexpected present in the bush. He released her and resumed the task of cleaning up.

"If you have another trash bag, I'll help you," Annie said.

"That sounds like one heck of a deal." He handed her one of the plastic bags. As they worked, Annie chattered about the party and the presents she'd received. As Jonathon listened to her he felt an odd regret, that at the end of the day when Annie was tucked into bed, there would be nobody for him to share his thoughts and feelings with about the special day.

"Daddy?" Annie sat down on one of the swings and looked at him expectantly. "Don't you think it would be nice if I had a baby brother or a sister?"

Jonathon stopped what he was doing and sat down in the swing next to his daughter. "Honey, I've explained all of this to you before. You can't get a brother or a sister until I get a wife."

Annie kicked her legs, moving her swing gently back and forth. "Megan says that babies grow from seeds. Why can't you go buy the seeds and we'll just grow a baby?"

"Well, because baby seeds grow in their mother's tummies. So we have to have a mother before we can have a baby. And the way to get a mother is for me to get a wife."

Annie frowned, her swing coming to a sudden halt. She eyed Jonathon, her frown deepening. "You aren't doing a very good job at finding one," she admonished him.

"It's a tough one, pumpkin," he admitted. "It's going to take a very special woman to be my wife and your mother, and so far I just haven't been able to find her."

"You have to look harder, Daddy."

They both turned as Rachel stepped out on the back patio. "Annie. A package was just delivered for you."

As Annie ran to retrieve the box from Rachel, Jonathon silently thanked his sister for the timely interruption. His daughter was beginning to be very demanding about the baby sister, baby brother issue.

Maybe he should go out with his sister's friend, Belinda. Who knew, perhaps Belinda was the woman he'd been waiting for, the one who would fulfill both his dreams and Annie's.

"Daddy, it's an angel," Annie exclaimed as she opened the package and withdrew a doll. "It's from Grandma, Daddy. I know it's from Grandma."

Jonathon got up from the swing and joined his daughter and his sister on the porch. "Honey, you know Grandma is in heaven. She couldn't have sent you the doll."

"But she did," Annie protested. "I know she did." She hugged the angel doll close to her heart.

"Look, here's a note." Rachel withdrew a piece of lavender paper from the box and handed it to Jonathon. Curious, he opened it and began to read aloud.

"Dear Annie,

Your grandmother asked me to send this doll to you for your birthday. Your grandmother is very busy in heaven.

She's in charge of halos and makes sure that they always shine. But she wanted you to know that she loves you very much. She's assigned me to be a sort of angel especially for you right here on earth, so you can write to me anytime. I hope you have a wonderful sixth birthday party.

Love, Mary."

Jonathon finished reading and looked first at his daughter, then at his sister. "There's a post office box number here."

"I told you it was from Grandma," Annie exclaimed, and hugged the angel doll close to her chest once again.

Rachel looked at Jonathon curiously, and he knew before the night was over he'd have to explain to his sister about the balloon they had released.

It was much later that evening when he finally got a chance to talk to Rachel alone. Annie was in bed, and all remnants of the birthday party had been cleaned up.

"So, who's this Mary?" Rachel asked as she poured them each a cup of coffee.

Jonathon shrugged. "You've got me. I imagine she found our balloon." At Rachel's look of puzzlement, he quickly explained about releasing the balloon to heaven. "I guess Annie's letter touched this Mary's heart, so she decided to respond."

"What a wonderful thing," Rachel replied, stirring her coffee thoughtfully. "It's not too often in this day and age that somebody takes the time to do something like this." She hesitated a moment, then gazed at him slyly. "Now, that sounds like the sort of woman you need to pursue."

Jonathon shrugged. "Oh, I don't know. She's probably some lonely old woman who doesn't have any grandchildren of her own."

"You don't know that. Maybe she's a young, gorgeous woman who just happens to have a wonderful heart."

"I doubt it," he replied, rising to top off Rachel's cup of coffee. He couldn't imagine a young, gorgeous woman who would take the time to see to a child's emotional needs. He felt certain that Mary was either an old woman or happily married.

"So, about the picnic I arranged for you and Belinda tomorrow at the zoo... Are you still going to go?"

Jonathon returned her smile, then stifled a yawn with the back of his hand. "If I don't agree, are you going to stay here and bug me until I do?"

"Absolutely."

"Then I'll save us both the hassle and agree right now. Besides, I'm too tired to argue with you."

Rachel laughed. "After the day you put in, you deserve to be tired." She finished her coffee and opened her purse. She handed him a slip of paper. "Here's Belinda's address. Remember, she's expecting you and Annie at noon. I'll get out of here and let you get a good night's sleep. I don't want you to be cranky tomorrow."

Jonathon walked with her to the front door. "Thanks, Rachel, for all your help today. I don't know how I would have coped without you."

"It was a wonderful party, Jonathon. You did a terrific job." Rachel reached up and touched her brother's cheek affectionately. "Annie is a lucky little girl to have you for a dad."

"No, I'm the lucky one to have her." He leaned over and gave his sister a kiss on her cheek. "Drive safe." He watched as Rachel got into her car, then disappeared down the block.

He closed the door and locked it, then went immediately to Annie's room to check on her before going to his own bed. He stood in the doorway of his daughter's room, a smile curving his lips as he gazed at the blond-haired sprite.

She was fast asleep, the angel doll clutched tightly against her. Annie was the one good thing that had come from his brief, miserable marriage to a beautiful woman who had wanted no commitments and no responsibility. The marriage had lasted exactly a year, at which time Katherine had informed him that she wasn't having fun anymore and wanted out. And she'd gotten out, taking nothing with her and leaving behind a three-month-old baby and a man who was more relieved than bitter. He'd been sorry when he'd heard of Katherine's death, but also somehow relieved that the selfish party girl would never have another opportunity to hurt Annie.

He'd made a mistake when he'd married Katherine, and he didn't want to make a second mistake. He had too much at stake; not only his own heart, but Annie's as well. It was important he not do that again.

He left Annie's doorway and went into his bedroom, struck by the utter silence of the house. Though the quiet should have made him happy, it was a lonely kind of silence instead. He undressed and got into bed, wishing there was somebody's head resting on the pillow next to his, somebody's passion waiting for him to embrace her, make love to her.

He lay on his back, watching the moonlight painting patterns on the ceiling. He wondered if Mary knew the same kind of loneliness that he did?

The yearning to make that special soul connection with another?

Frowning, he turned over on his side. The mysterious Mary was probably a blue-haired old woman who lived with a houseful of cats. Still, no matter her age, she'd shown a special kind of heart. It was the kind of heart he'd love to find in a woman, the kind of heart that could make him fall in love again. The thought both comforted him and terrified him. Never again did he want to give the kind of power he'd given to Katherine; he'd given her his love and been burned badly.

He shoved thoughts of Mary aside and instead focused on his date the next day. Belinda Currothers. Who knew, maybe she was the one he'd been waiting to find.

3

———◆———

Belinda Currothers bounded out of her house before Jonathon's car had come to a full stop in her driveway. A big-boned woman with coffee-colored eyes and reddish brown hair, she wasn't exactly Jonathon's physical type. However, her smile was wide and her energy filled the car as she stored the large picnic basket in the back seat, then slid into the passenger side.

"Hi. You must be Jonathon." She flashed him a quick smile, then turned and looked at Annie, her smile widening. "And you must be Annie. Your Aunt Rachel told me all about you. She told me you love chocolate chip cookies and roasted marshmallows, and guess what I brought as part of our picnic lunch?"

"Chocolate chip cookies and marshmallows?" Annie replied.

"Right! Your Aunt Rachel also told me you were smart. So, what is your favorite zoo animal? I think I like the monkeys best."

As Jonathon drove toward the zoo, Belinda and Annie filled the car with laughter and conversation, talking about favorite animals and their love of Kansas City's Swope Park Zoo.

He was aware of Belinda's scent, not especially feminine, but clean and pleasant. Clad in a pair of white shorts and a white-and-red striped blouse, she exuded the aura of good health and vitality.

Normally Jonathon preferred women a little less hearty, a little more feminine, but as he heard Annie's sweet giggles, he consciously shoved aside his personal tastes and reservations. If Annie liked Belinda, that just might be enough for him.

"Rachel told me you're a teacher," Jonathon said as they got out of the car and headed for the admission gates of the zoo.

Belinda nodded, smiling as Annie danced around them, her excitement contagious. "Yes, I teach second grade. I adore children. I'd love to have about a dozen of my own." She paused a moment, then continued, "My gynecologist says I have the hips of a natural child-bearer."

Jonathon blinked in surprise. "Uh...that's great," he replied, unsure how else to answer and hoping she didn't share more of what her gynecologist had told her in the privacy of an examination.

He sighed in silent relief as he paid for their tickets and Annie chattered about the animals they would be seeing. "I like polar bears and tigers and the monkeys, too," she said to Belinda. "I like all the animals," she finished, her blue eyes sparkling with excitement.

The afternoon progressed pleasantly. They walked in leisure from one man-made habitat to the next, visiting first the African veldt then the steamy inside display of the reptiles and amphibious creatures.

He and Belinda visited off and on, interrupted frequently by Annie's observations and delight. He learned that Belinda loved the great outdoors, belonged to a rock-climbing group and was a vegetarian.

Watching a football game from box seats was about as outdoorsy as Jonathon got. The only rocks he cared about were in the bottom of his drink glass, and there was nothing he enjoyed better than a big juicy steak grilled to perfection. Still, as he witnessed how much Annie seemed to enjoy Belinda's company, he thought perhaps he might be able to compromise. Certainly he was willing to give it a whirl, for Annie's sake.

At three o'clock, with half the zoo still left to see, they decided to get their picnic lunch and take a break. Jonathon carried the basket Belinda had packed to a picnic table beneath a shady tree.

"Ah, a perfect spot," Belinda said as he set the basket down. "Rachel told me you're a pilot," she said as she began to unload their picnic. "That must be so exciting, flying off to exotic places and being up among the clouds."

"It was, although I no longer fly commercially. I'm now teaching courses at the community college." He sat down on the bench, watching as Annie ran toward a nearby swing set. "I needed to make some adjustments in my life after my mother died. Now I'm home most of the time so I can take care of Annie."

"So we're both teachers." Belinda smiled as if pleased to find some common ground.

He nodded. "Teaching is a relatively new experience for me, but I'm enjoying it."

"I find it very rewarding. I can't imagine doing anything else." She smiled at him shyly. "Although I must confess, I spend so much time around seven-year-olds, I worry I'll lose the ability to talk to adults."

Jonathon smiled, finding her momentary shyness rather appealing. "As far as I'm concerned, you're doing just fine," he assured her.

She flashed him a bright smile, then took the last item out of the basket and set it on the table. "Well, it looks like we're ready to eat."

Jonathon nodded and turned in the direction of the swing set. "Annie, come on and eat some lunch."

The little girl came running, her pigtails bouncing on her shoulders. She crawled up on the bench next to her father and grinned at Belinda. "I like her, Daddy. Can we marry her and plant a seed?"

Jonathon felt the blush that warmed his face at his daughter's words. He offered a sickly smile to Belinda, his brain searching for something to say, a way to explain his daughter's words.

Belinda laughed. "I won't even ask," she said.

He sighed gratefully. "Let's eat and talk about it later, okay, sweetheart?" he said to his daughter.

As the rest of the afternoon wore on, Jonathon couldn't help but be impressed with the rapport between Annie and Belinda. Belinda patiently answered a myriad of questions about each animal they saw, never seeming to tire of Annie or her endless curiosity.

As they came to the monkey island, Jonathon found a bench and sat down while the two females observed and teased the monkeys. They had seen every animal the park had to offer, ridden the train twice and petted everything that could be touched in the petting park area. He was exhausted, but Belinda and Annie didn't seem to be wearing down at all.

He watched Belinda, trying not to notice that her calf and thigh muscles put his to shame. Not that he was in bad shape, but rock-climbing obviously built strong muscles.

He tried to imagine those legs wrapped around him. She could probably squeeze the life out of him. He shoved those thoughts away, reminding himself that Annie liked Belinda.

Belinda might not be the physical type that caused his blood to roar hot, but she was nice and pleasant and he was more than aware of the fact that he could no longer simply please himself where women were concerned. Whoever he brought into his life would also become a major part of Annie's life.

He could make himself be more attracted to Belinda if she was good for Annie. He could forget that he liked petite, feminine women who preferred Bach to rocks. Yes, perhaps he could force himself to fall in love with Belinda if Annie loved her and wanted her for a mother. She had a nice mouth, and it couldn't be unpleasant kissing her. He supposed if he tried hard enough, he could probably even work up some enthusiasm about kissing Belinda.

As he watched his little girl and the teacher, pointing and laughing at the monkey's antics, he thought of the mysterious guardian angel, Mary. He definitely needed to send a thank-you note to the post office box number she'd provided. He should tell her that Annie had adored the stuffed angel, had in fact slept with it all night long. Mary had obviously given the gift much thought and had gone to a lot of trouble to choose such a precious, perfect gift. Better yet, he would help Annie write a thank-you note. It really should come from her.

As laughter filled the air, he looked back at Belinda and Annie. Belinda had her tongue shoved against the inside of her lower lip, apparently doing a monkey imitation. Annie giggled and attempted to emulate her.

As Jonathon watched the two jumping and gyrating, making monkey noises and scratching, he again tried to imagine himself kissing Belinda. No matter how hard he concentrated on bringing the image alive in his mind, it wouldn't gel. In his heart, he knew this was something he couldn't get past.

He sighed, realizing he'd just learned an important fact of life. Once you've seen a woman acting like a monkey, it would be impossible to think of her romantically.

"No." Mary shook her head to emphasize her one-word answer to Lucinda.

"Oh, come on, it will be fun," Lucinda protested. "It's ladies' night and drinks are only a dollar apiece. We don't even have to stay that late."

"You know I don't drink, and why would I want to go to a nightclub on ladies' night?"

"Because ladies' night always draws in the men. Honey, it's a wonderful place to meet Mr. Right." Lucinda flopped down on the sofa next to Mary.

"After my date last night I've just about decided Cowpoke is the only male I want to spend the rest of my life with."

"That bad, huh?" Lucinda commiserated, then grinned. "That's what you get when you go out on a date set up by your mother."

"Oh, Herman wasn't so bad, he just wasn't my type."

"Herman?" Lucinda caught a giggle in a cupped hand, then sobered as Mary glared at her. "All the more reason to hit Sebastian's Nightclub with me tonight. No strings, no commitments, just a couple of hours of looking over the men and seeing if anyone strikes your fancy. Come on, Mary. Live a little. Tonight might be the night you meet Mr. Prince Charming."

"I hope so, because I'm getting really tired of kissing all of the toads," Mary replied dryly, and got up off the sofa. "Give me ten minutes to change my clothes."

As Mary changed, Lucinda kept up a running monologue detailing all the attributes of Sebastian's, her favorite singles' club. Although Mary knew she should spend tonight preparing for a new week of work, catch up on her sleep or clean the bathroom, a shiver of excitement danced up her spine as she slipped into a pair of black slacks and a gray silk blouse.

Maybe Lucinda was right. Perhaps tonight she'd meet the man who'd share her dreams and her life. She certainly wasn't going to meet him by staying alone in her apartment sleeping or cleaning bathrooms.

If you're shopping for a man, you should at least go to the store, she told her reflection in the mirror. She ran a brush through her hair and added a dab of pale pink lipstick, then hurried back into the living room where Lucinda paced impatiently.

She frowned as she eyed Mary critically. "Don't you have anything brighter? A little sexier? You look like you're going to a funeral instead of a nightclub." She didn't give Mary a chance to reply. "Oh, well, never mind. We'd better get moving. On Sunday nights people tend to pair off early in the evening because the bar closes early."

Mary had no idea what to expect, but was pleasantly surprised by the interior of Sebastian's. Brass-and-glass tables and chairs surrounded a small, shiny dance floor. The music wasn't so loud it inhibited conversation. Plants and greenery artfully placed created an intimacy that was immediately appealing.

Even though it was only a little past seven, the place was already jumping. Couples crowded the dance floor and the stools at the bar were filled. She and Lucinda found an empty table near the bar and sat down, and they were almost immediately greeted by a waitress.

Lucinda ordered a gin and tonic and Mary ordered a soda. When the waitress had served them, Mary gazed around in unabashed curiosity. Nightclubs had never been Mary's thing and it had been years since she'd been in one. The women looked as if they had dressed to outdo one another, each one sparkling and more vibrant than the next. Mary felt like a moth amid butterflies in her muted colors and dab of lipstick.

"Everyone looks so young," she said to Lucinda, who was making eyes with a hunk on the dance floor.

"Honey, most of them are young. At least you know for sure if they're in here they're over the age of consent."

Mary sighed. She didn't want somebody she'd have to raise. As her mother was so fond of reminding her, she was almost thirty, and the idea of dating a twenty-one-year-old didn't exactly cause her hormones to sit up and dance with joy.

She nursed her soda, watching the gyrating hunk make meaningful eye contact with Lucinda. She figured by the time the next dance started she'd be sitting alone. Terrific. She should have stayed home and scrubbed her bathtub.

Sure enough, when the music ended and a new song began, the hunk came to their table and asked Lucinda to dance. Mary watched her friend, admiring Lucinda's ease. As Lucinda danced she talked and laughed with her partner. Where Mary found the dating game painful, Lucinda found it exciting, stimulating.

Mary shifted her attention from the dance floor to the bar, surprised to meet the gaze of a nice-looking man sitting alone. He smiled and nodded. She returned his smile, then stared down into her glass. At least he didn't look like a teenybopper. A touch of gray dusted his sideburns and silver strands glistened in his hair. Definitely not a youngster, but not too old, either. She looked at him again, and this time he lifted his glass in a gesture of friendliness.

"Whew, that was fun." Lucinda flopped back down in the seat across from Mary, flashing the hunk a flirtatious smile as he moved in the direction of the bar. "His name is Gary. Isn't he cute?"

Mary nodded. "There's a guy at the bar giving me the eye," she said.

"Where?" Lucinda casually shifted her position so she could see. "Oh, you don't mean the older guy in the blue suit, do you?"

"Yes, that's him."

"Don't smile at him, don't even look at him," Lucinda warned, then giggled. "He's a jerk. The regular girls who come in here call him Prophylactic Paul."

Mary stared at her friend. She didn't want to know. She wasn't about to ask. "Good grief. Why?" The question slipped out unbidden.

Lucinda giggled. "His name really is Paul something-or-other, but he got his nickname because he carries condoms in his pockets. All kinds and colors. Likes to give a woman her choice." Lucinda laughed again. "Some men carry business cards. Paul carries condoms."

"That's gross," Mary replied, wishing she could take back the smiles she'd cast his way.

"There's somebody gross in every bar. The trick is to learn to recognize him at first glance."

Mary bit her tongue. She didn't intend to ever go to enough bars to learn to discern the creeps at first glance. In fact, she couldn't wait to get out of this place. Suddenly she felt too old, too out of it, too sane to be in here at all. "Lucinda, this was a mistake. This kind of thing just isn't for me." She stood up and grabbed her purse. "Don't worry, I'll catch a cab home." Before Lucinda could talk her out of leaving, Mary ran for the nearest exit.

As the taxi drove her down the streets taking her home, Mary stared out the window, noting that everywhere she looked were couples. Couples in front of the movie theaters, couples sitting in restaurants, couples walking hand in hand down the street. The world seemed to love pairs. Buy one, get one free. Two for a dollar. Two for the price of one. Oh, yes, things worked best in pairs. Would she ever find the half to make her whole?

She closed her eyes, her thoughts shooting to the little girl named Annie. Had she gotten the angel doll in time for her birthday party? Had she liked it?

Oh, it would be nice to meet a man who needed a mother for his children, a man who wouldn't care about adding more to his family. A man who wouldn't care that she would never have children of her own.

Of course, Annie had made it clear in her letter that she wanted a brother or sister. And Mary was certain a man who had aided his child in sending a balloon to heaven would see to it that she got her wish for siblings.

She sighed, suddenly very, very depressed.

* * *

"It was a fun day, wasn't it?" Jonathon said as he pulled into Belinda's driveway. It was just after ten o'clock. They had seen everything the zoo had to offer, then had finished the evening at a local ice cream parlor. Annie had fallen asleep in the back seat, her face decorated with cotton candy, chocolate sundae and a happy smile.

"It was a terrific day," Belinda agreed. Jonathon gathered up the picnic basket and together they got out of the car. "You've got quite a daughter there, Jonathon. So bright and fun."

He nodded and handed her the basket as they reached her front door. "She is quite a kid. The best." Belinda's features looked softer, more attractive in the muted light from her porch. "She certainly took to you easily."

"She's a very likable child." Belinda unlocked her front door. "Well, thanks." She turned to go inside, stopping as Jonathon called her name. She turned back to him.

"How about a movie later this week?" he said. "I could get a baby-sitter for Annie and we could spend a little adult time together."

Belinda placed a hand on his arm. "Jonathon, I adore Annie. And you're a very attractive man, but to tell you the truth, I don't think it would work between the two of us." She smiled, her features a lot less pleasant than they'd been moments before. "To tell you the truth, you do nothing for me." She gave him a final pat on the cheek, then disappeared into her house.

For a long moment Jonathon stood on the porch, trying to figure out exactly what had just happened. He had the distinct feeling of being dumped. And yet instead of being unhappy, he felt elated.

He grinned, feeling a little silly as he walked back to his car. He'd been so self-righteous, thinking he'd suffered through another date with Belinda even though she wasn't his type—all because Annie seemed so taken with her. He'd never considered Belinda wouldn't be taken with him. The thought never even crossed his mind.

As he got back into the car, Annie stirred in the back seat. She sat up and rubbed her eyes. "Are we gonna marry Belinda, Daddy?" she asked, her voice husky with the remnants of sleep.

"No, pumpkin. We're not going to marry Belinda."

Annie sighed, a sigh far too big for such a little girl. "Oh, Daddy, are we ever gonna get married and plant seeds?"

"I don't know, honey. I honestly don't know." Backing the car up, Jonathon turned it around and pointed it toward home.

4

"Daddy, I gotta sore throat."

Annie's voice pierced through the fog of Jonathon's sleep, pulling him from a wonderful dream involving a busty blonde, himself and a can of non-dairy whipped topping.

He cracked open one eye and peered at the little girl standing next to his bed, her angel doll clutched tightly in her arms. He shot a glance at his alarm clock. It was 6:00 a.m. He sat up and rubbed his face, the lingering memory of the voluptuous blonde fading away. "Come here and let me feel your forehead."

Annie moved closer to the bed and Jonathon placed a kiss on the top of her head. He frowned as he felt the heat of a fever radiating from her. "Here, sweetheart, jump into bed and let me see if I can find a thermometer." He got up and helped her into the king-size bed, then padded out of the room and into the kitchen where he thought he'd last seen the thermometer in the bottom of a junk drawer.

Shoving aside little screwdrivers, masking tape, scraps of paper and a ball of string, he tried to keep his worry at bay. Annie had always been blessedly healthy. The few times she'd been ill, his mother had handled it, taking her to the doctor, getting the prescription and nursing the little girl. But Regina Taylor was no longer there to take care of Annie.

"Ah-ha," he muttered triumphantly as he spied the blue thermometer case. He carried it back into the bedroom and withdrew the thermometer. He shook it down and placed it beneath Annie's tongue.

Turning on the bedside lamp, he gazed at his daughter, noting her cheeks were flushed and her eyes appeared overbright. He wasn't surprised when the thermometer registered her fever at 102°. He smoothed a strand of her damp hair off her forehead. "Your throat hurt really bad?"

She nodded. "Really bad, Daddy. Like I swallowed a porcupine."

He smiled sympathetically. "You hang tight right here. I'll be back in a flash."

She nodded again, her eyes drifting closed. Jonathon went out to the kitchen, worry whispering through him. He had no clue what to do. Starve a cold, feed a fever? Feed a cold, starve a fever? How high could a fever go before it was dangerous? Was

102 close to brain-frying temperature? He didn't even know which doctor Annie usually saw.

Despite the early hour, he didn't hesitate calling Rachel. The phone rang four times before his sister's groggy voice muttered a hoarse hello.

"Annie's sick," Jonathon said without preamble.

"What's wrong with her?" The sleepiness instantly left Rachel's voice.

"A sore throat and a fever."

"How high is the fever?"

"It's 102. That's high, isn't it? What should I do? Should I take her to the emergency room? Do you know what doctor Mother used?" Jonathon could hear the rising anxiety in his own voice.

"Jonathon, the first thing you need to do is calm down. Children often run those kinds of temperatures. Make sure she drinks plenty of fluids and give her some children's cold medicine. If she's not better by this afternoon, you might need to take her into the doctor."

"Which doctor?" Jonathon sighed. "I feel so helpless. I feel guilty that for so long I just depended on Mom to take care of things."

"Jonathon, Mom made it easy for you to depend on her. She wanted to do for you and Annie. Don't beat yourself up about it. You're a wonderful father and Annie is lucky to have you. Now, Mom always used Dr. Burwell. He's in the south part of the city. I've got the number here someplace.''

There was a long pause and Jonathon heard the shuffling of papers and the opening of various drawers.

''Okay, here it is.''

Jonathon wrote down the number, thanked his sister, then hung up and went back into his bedroom. Annie had fallen back asleep. For a long moment he merely gazed at his daughter, as always his heart expanding with love.

There were times a residual stab of bitterness pierced through him when he thought of his failed marriage. However, he could never be sorry he'd married Katherine, because without the marriage there would be no Annie.

Rachel had been right, his mother had made it too easy for him to allow her to be the major caretaker for Annie. And during that time, Jonathon hadn't realized how much of Annie's life he'd been missing. The responsibility for raising Annie weighed heavy in his heart, but it was tempered with a joy he hadn't thought possible.

He sat down on the edge of the bed, his gaze still on the sleeping child. He wanted to give her some juice, as Rachel had suggested, but was reluctant to wake her up. She appeared to be sleeping peacefully and the juice could wait.

What he really wished was that he could give her a mother, a woman to nurture her as only a female could. Annie wanted a mommy, and a full family with a brother or a sister, and Jonathon feared it was the one wish of hers that would be most difficult to fulfill.

He leaned down and lightly kissed her forehead, then got up and went into the kitchen, needing some coffee while he decided what he would do about his class that day.

He didn't want to take Annie to the baby-sitter if she was sick. He only had one afternoon class. He could cancel it if Annie didn't feel better.

By nine o'clock, Annie's temperature hadn't come down and Jonathon made two calls, one to cancel his afternoon class and the other to make an appointment at Dr. Burwell's office.

At one o'clock he and Annie drove to the doctor's office. Jonathon's worry had increased throughout the course of the morning. Annie was unusually lethargic and had refused to eat anything because it hurt too much when she swallowed.

"Okay, princess, here we are," he said as he pulled into a parking space in front of the doctor's office.

Annie didn't move from her seat. "Am I gonna get a shot?" she asked, her bottom lip quivering.

Jonathon bit back his automatic inclination to tell her no and instead frowned thoughtfully. "Hmm, I suppose it's possible," he told her truthfully. "We'll have to wait and see what the doctor says." He unbuckled her seat belt. "Come on, honey. You can bring your angel doll with you."

"Her name is Mary," Annie said as they walked toward the office building. "Because that's the name of the lady who Grandma picked to be my friend."

"That's nice, Annie," Jonathon replied, reminding himself to write a thank-you note to the mysterious Mary.

All thoughts of thank-you notes and mystery women fled from his head as he and Annie entered the chaos of the parents' waiting room.

Every kid in Kansas City must be sick and in the room, he thought as he made his way toward the reception desk. He wanted to pick Annie up in his arms, stick her in a plastic bubble, shield her from all the other sniffling, sneezing, coughing, germ-spreading kids.

"Hi, Annie Taylor is here. She has an appointment," he said to the brown-haired receptionist. She stared at him as if he were an escaped patient from an asylum. Then, as if aware she was staring, she cast her gaze downward toward the appointment book, her face flushed a becoming pink.

"Annie Taylor? Yes, I've got her right here. If you'll just have a seat, the doctor should be with you shortly."

He nodded, wishing she'd look up at him again. She had the nicest blue eyes...eyes as blue as a cloudless spring sky. But she didn't, and as Annie tugged on his hand, he led her to a seat and together they sat to wait for the doctor.

Annie Taylor. Mary felt as if she'd been suckerpunched. Her Annie Taylor. If the name hadn't been enough to shake her up, the fact that the little girl hugged a very familiar angel doll against her chest proved that the sweet little blonde was, indeed, her Annie Taylor.

She smiled to herself. Funny how in such a brief time she'd begun to identify Annie possessively. Her Annie Taylor.

Rechecking the appointment book, Mary realized the call for the appointment must have come in while she was on her morning break.

Sneaking a peek at the child, Mary realized she didn't have to worry whether Annie liked her gift. Even though she'd only had the doll a couple of days, it was obvious the doll was loved. A bent halo and crooked wings attested to hugs and kisses, cuddles and loving.

Mary drank in the features of the child, pleased that from now on her musings about the little girl would include long blond hair and vivid blue eyes, a pert little nose and a sweet smile. She sat on her daddy's lap as he read quietly to her from one of the children's books that were scattered around the room for that purpose.

Her gaze drifted from Annie to Annie's father, and a crazy fluttering tickled her stomach. Attractive, with dark hair that fell carelessly across the top of his forehead, he was clad in casual slacks and a pale blue dress shirt. The sleeves were rolled up, exposing strong forearms lightly dusted with dark hair.

It had been a long time since the mere sight of a man created butterflies in her stomach. The last time had been when she'd first spotted her cowboy standing outside her dry cleaners.

Still, all the stomach flutters in the world didn't change the fact that Annie's father was looking for a wife who could give his daughter a brother or sister. He was certainly attractive enough that it shouldn't be a problem to find a volunteer for the job.

"Mary, I need the file for Jennifer Tompkins." Lucinda's voice held the kind of impatience that let Mary know it wasn't the first time she'd spoken.

"Sorry." She flushed and pulled her gaze away from Annie and her father. "Here you are." She handed Lucinda the requested file.

"Today is not the day to pull one of your space cadet imitations," Lucinda teased, looking pointedly at the crowded waiting room. As Dr. Burwell bellowed, Lucinda took off, running back to the examination rooms.

As Annie and her dad waited for their appointment, Mary tried to keep her attention focused on her work, but she found herself sneaking surreptitious glances at the pair. Part of her wanted to jump up and say, 'Hey, it's me. I'm the Mary who sent you the doll.'" The other part of her hugged the secret close to her heart.

Besides, what good could come from her confessing who she was? She had no place in Annie's future. After all, she'd only intended to be a temporary, mysterious part of it until the little girl had worked through her grief from her grandmother's death. No, best to keep it a secret, one that would warm her on cold, lonely nights.

Relief coursed through her when finally at two-thirty Annie was called into one of the examination rooms and she and her father disappeared from Mary's sight.

With a lull in the patient load, Mary left her desk and straightened up the waiting room, putting puzzles back together, placing books back on the appropriate shelves and disposing of candy and gum wrappers.

She'd just sat back down when Annie came down the hallway toward her. The little girl stopped next to Mary's desk. "I gotta shot," she exclaimed. "And I didn't cry, so Dr. Burwell said I could come out here and get a lollipop.''

"I have a whole drawer full of lollipops for brave little girls," Mary replied, fighting the impulse to gather Annie on her lap, smell the sweet scent of her hair. "What kind do you like?" she asked as she pulled the large bag out of her drawer.

"You got watermelon? That's my very favorite."

Mary filed away that information for future presents from a grandmother in heaven. "What a nice doll," she said, pointing to the angel doll hugged tight against Annie's chest.

"Her name is Mary," Annie replied.

Mary's heart filled with warmth. She was so glad she'd been the one to find the red balloon, so pleased that fate had allowed her a special, magical place in this little girl's life. "My name is Mary, too," she said, pointing to her name tag.

Annie smiled. "I've got another friend named Mary. She's seven years old." Annie leaned closer to Mary and whispered, "And she's too bossy."

Mary laughed in delight, again wishing she could snuggle the child on her lap, whisper her secret in Annie's ear.

"Could I have one more lollipop?" Annie asked. "It's not for me," she added, as if she'd been told many times by adults not to be greedy.

"Is it for your father?" Mary asked, pulling the bag of candy out once again.

Annie giggled, a wondrous sound that seemed to come from her toes. "No, my daddy doesn't eat lollipops. We're trying to find a mommy, and when we do we're gonna plant a seed and grow a baby brother or sister who'll need a lollipop, too. I'll save it for when the baby's old enough."

Again a weight of depression plummeted into the bottom of Mary's heart. She could pretend that fate had given her a chance to be a part of Annie's and her father's life, but as usual it was just a case of fate spitting in her face. "Here you are," she said as she handed Annie another candy.

"Tell the pretty lady thank you, Annie."

Mary looked up to see Annie's dad, a sexy smile on his handsome face. Immediately she felt the blush that swept warmth into her cheeks. Annie murmured her thanks and he held out his hand toward Mary. "I'm Jonathon Taylor, Annie's dad."

"Mary Wellington," she replied, vaguely disappointed as he released her hand. His grip had been firm, his skin warm, and the brief contact had increased the beating of her heart.

"We need to make another appointment for next week," he said.

Mary nodded and focused on her appointment book. She was aware of his scent, a pleasant mixture of spice and musk. His eyes flirted with her, their gray color warming her as effectively as flannel pajamas on a cold night. "Would next Wednesday be all right? Nine o'clock?"

"Perfect," he replied, smiling the sexy grin that caused her heart to once again step up its rhythm.

Mary quickly wrote out an appointment card and handed it to him. "Just a reminder card," she explained.

"Thanks." He tucked it into his pocket. "I'd better get this sick child home," he said as Annie leaned against his leg.

"I hope it's nothing too serious," Mary said.

"Dr. Burwell said it's probably strep throat. He took a culture and we'll know for sure by tomorrow."

"I think I accidently swallowed a porcupine," Annie quipped.

Rich and deep, Jonathon's laughter mingled with Mary's as Annie grinned, obviously pleased she'd made the two adults laugh. "The antibiotics should get rid of that pesky porcupine," he said to his daughter. Taking Annie's hand, he turned to leave.

Annie stopped him, looking back at Mary. "Daddy promised me some ice cream. You wanna come with us to get some?"

"Honey, you're probably contagious and shouldn't be out," Mary replied.

"I'll pick up some ice cream on the way home," Jonathon said, then smiled at Mary. "But maybe another time you'd like to get some ice cream with us."

Oh, she wanted to say yes. She would have loved to spend more time with Annie and her very attractive father. But what was the point? Where could it possibly lead? She floundered for a diplomatic way to say no.

"Annie and I will look forward to it," he said. Before she could reply he flashed her that wicked grin, then he and Annie left the office.

Mary stared at the door for a long moment, fighting the impulse to run after them, tell them she'd love to get ice cream with them. Anytime. Anywhere.

She stared down at the appointment book, tears blurring her vision. Sometimes fate was cruel.

"The doctor says you have to get plenty of sleep," Jonathon said as he tucked Annie into bed earlier than usual that night.

"And that will make my throat feel better?" Annie asked.

Jonathon nodded, then leaned over and kissed his daughter good-night. "Sweet dreams, princess." He shut off the light and left the room.

Drifting into the living room, he poured himself a glass of wine and took it out on the patio. Night had fallen and the air was rife with the scent of spring flowers fully bloomed. What was it about spring and a man's fancy? He couldn't remember but suspected it had to do with too much testosterone and the need to procreate... or at least practice the act of procreation.

He sank down on a patio chair and sipped the wine, his thoughts drifting to the woman in the doctor's office. Mary Wellington. There had been a sweetness to her smile, a spark in her eyes that had prompted the spontaneous invitation to have ice cream with them. He'd been surprisingly disappointed when she hadn't taken them up on the offer.

Win some, lose some, he thought, then frowned. Unfortunately, he seemed to be losing a lot lately. Oh, well, perhaps next week when he took Annie back in to the office, he'd follow up and invite Mary to get ice cream or have dinner with them.

What he didn't understand about himself was why the women he was most drawn to were gorgeous, self-absorbed, selfish women who would make the worst possible mother material?

He finished his wine and stood up, suddenly remembering he had a thank-you note to write. Funny how two Marys had made an impression on him in a single week. He'd write one now, and perhaps next Wednesday when they went in for Annie's follow-up appointment, he'd ask the other one out.

5

⟵◆⟶

"Herman!" Mary stared in surprise at the man on her doorstep. "What are you doing here?" It was Wednesday afternoon and normally Mary would be at work.

She'd done something completely uncharacteristic and called in sick, unwilling to face Jonathon and Annie Taylor again. She'd been afraid he'd make good on his promise and invite her to get ice cream. Even more, she feared her resolve not to go would melt beneath the warmth of his ash-colored eyes.

It was crazy how much the handsome man and his charming little daughter had invaded her thoughts. Crazy, and dangerous.

"I spoke to your mother this morning and she said you were home sick." He smiled, the gesture painfully eager. "I had the afternoon off, so I brought you some chicken soup." He offered her a bowl of what appeared to be homemade soup covered with plastic wrap.

"Oh, Herman, that's so sweet, but you shouldn't have." She wished he hadn't. She really wished he hadn't. She opened the door wider to allow him in, feeling like a fraud.

She smelled her mother's hand in this. She should never have told her mother she was staying home sick. Wondering if she could get away with murdering her mother, she motioned Herman in. Who would possibly miss a fifty-five-year-old busybody?

She carried the soup into the kitchen, Herman at her heels. "It's my mother's special recipe," he explained. "She swears it will fix whatever ails you. The secret is garlic... lots of garlic."

Garlic? The thought of lots of garlic mixed with chicken and noodles caused her stomach to buck and roll.

"You're close to your mother?" Mary asked, pointing him to a chair at the table. Although she'd prefer to hurry him on his way, she couldn't help but be touched by his thoughtfulness. She'd be nice, share conversation over a cup of coffee and then hurry him on his way.

"Oh, yes, Mother is my best friend," Herman replied, an answer that somehow didn't surprise Mary. She only wished that "Mother" would cut that dreadful hair between Herman's eyes. "Of course, it wasn't always that way. But as you get older, you get wiser."

"Coffee?" she asked.

"Please." He leaned back in his chair and looked around. "You've got a nice place here, Mary. Cheerful and homey. My place lacks a woman's touch, but this is all real nice."

"Thanks." Mary set his coffee in front of him, then joined him at the table. She was aware of his eyes lingering on her. He had nice eyes, but they couldn't compete with the sexy gray ones of Jonathon Taylor.

Stop it, she reprimanded herself; Jonathon Taylor was taboo where she was concerned. She and Jonathon were like...like garlic and chicken soup...a crazy combination.

She focused again on Herman, trying desperately to like him. After all, he had grown children, wanted no more kids, and in that respect he was perfect marriage material for her.

"I had such a good time the other night," Herman said. "I even told Mother all about you. She's looking forward to meeting you soon." His face reddened slightly and he averted his gaze to the coffee in his cup. "I haven't been able to stop thinking about you."

Mary cleared her throat, unsure how to reply. Sorry, Herman, I haven't been thinking of you? Gosh, Herman, I'm glad I made such an impression? That's nice, Herman, but it's against my religion to date a man who has a hair between his eyes longer than the hair on my head? She choked and coughed, hoping Herman couldn't read her mind. "Sorry, swallowed wrong," she sputtered.

Herman smiled sympathetically. "Don't you hate when that happens?"

She nodded and took a sip of her coffee, hoping to slide through the awkward moment. "So, my mom told me you have a couple of grown children."

He nodded. "Three, although I must confess I'm not very close to them. Their mother and I divorced when they were fairly young and we just sort of lost touch. The divorce was quite unpleasant."

He shook his head. "Mother warned me before I ever married Glenda that she was a spiteful, nasty woman. Of course at the time I was young and impetuous and didn't listen. Now I pay attention to what Mother tells me."

"That's too bad...I mean that you aren't close to your kids," Mary replied, unable to imagine having children and not working hard to maintain a relationship with them.

Suddenly she wanted to be alone. She didn't want to be sharing coffee with a man who was sweet, but who would never be right for her. "Herman, I hate to be rude, but I'm really not feeling very well."

He frowned apologetically. "Of course, how thoughtless of me." He finished his coffee, then took the cup to the sink and rinsed it out. "Why don't I warm up that soup for you before I leave?" he asked.

"Oh, really, that's not necessary. I'll just pop it into the microwave later when I get hungry." She walked with him to the front door, touched by his offer to warm up the soup.

Really, he wasn't a bad sort. Certainly he was the first man who'd ever brought her chicken soup. "Thank you again, Herman, for stopping by and bringing the soup."

"Ah, it was nothing." He paused at the door, an eager smile once again curving his mouth. "How about a movie on Friday night?"

Her first inclination was to say no, but something about the puppy-dog eagerness on his face and the thought of his chicken soup made her relent. "Sure, a movie would be nice."

"Great! Why don't we plan on my picking you up at seven?"

"That would be fine." She watched as Herman walked down the sidewalk toward his car at the curb. What had possessed her to agree to another date? There was positively no magical spark with Herman, no chemistry whatsoever.

She closed the door and went back into the living room. Maybe chemistry was for teenagers. Maybe she was a fool to be expecting a racing pulse, a pounding heart and sweaty palms. Maybe when you reached almost thirty you traded away the desire for chemistry and instead focused on compatibility and common interests.

And maybe while in the movie Herman would fall asleep and Mary could grab a pair of tweezers and yank out that hair that bobbed and danced between his eyes. She grinned at the vision, then sighed, her thoughts shifting to Jonathon Taylor.

Now there was a man she could work up a little chemistry for. Even now, the memory of those flirtatious gray eyes and warm smile caused her heart to beat a little more rapidly, her palms to grow damp and her face to burn with internal heat.

A mental image of him formed in her head. The strong, bold features softened by a small cleft in his chin. Not only did he have gorgeous eyes, but he also had a pair of lips that looked perfect for kissing. She sighed and blinked to dispel his image.

Taking the day off because he and Annie had an appointment had been a childish way to avoid temptation, and she knew it wasn't an option the next time they had an appointment.

If he came back in and if he and Annie invited her to go with them for ice cream, she'd just have to be strong and decline. After all, nothing would be served in her being anything in their lives except a mysterious woman sending gifts from Grandma.

She jumped as the doorbell rang. Who could that be? Most of her friends knew she worked every day until five or six in the evening. Probably some sort of salesman. She stifled a groan as she saw her mother standing on the porch, wishing she'd never mentioned to her she was taking the day off. "Hi, Mom," she greeted the meticulously groomed woman.

"Hi, darling." Patricia kissed the air next to Mary's cheek, then swept past her with the regal bearing of a queen.

Mary closed the door with a sigh of resignation. She'd hoped to head her mother off at the pass, exchange a moment or two of pleasantries on the porch, then send her back on her way. "What are you doing here, Mom?" she asked as she followed the tall brunette into the kitchen.

"You mentioned you felt ill, so I thought I'd drop in and check on you." Patricia's face lit up as she spied the bowl of soup on the countertop. "Ah, I see Herman did stop by. He said he might." She sat down at the table, smugness playing at the corners of her lips. "Herman is quite smitten with you, my dear."

"Mom." The word escaped Mary on a sigh.

"You know he would make you a wonderful husband. Financially he's quite secure and you could certainly do a lot worse."

"Mother, I keep telling you to stop matchmaking, stop trying to push me into marriage."

"Somebody needs to push you. You aren't getting any younger. Trust me on this, my dear. Once you pass thirty, it's all downhill from there."

Mary sank down in the chair across from her mother. "Last night I dreamed I sent you on a plane trip around the world," she began.

"Oh, what a nice dream."

Mary nodded and smiled, deciding not to tell her mother the rest of the dream, that Patricia hadn't been sitting in first class, but instead was shoved in a steamer trunk and shipped from exotic port to exotic port, never to return to Kansas City again.

Patricia frowned again, her gaze sweeping her daughter from head to toe. "I hope you weren't wearing those sweats when Herman stopped by. Honestly, Mary, they aren't the most attractive items of clothing you own."

Mary looked down at the faded navy sweatshirt and pants. "But they are the most comfortable, and I wasn't exactly expecting company," she protested. "I didn't know you were going to tell Herman I was home sick, and I had no idea he would stop by unexpectedly." She inserted a finger in the ragged hole at her knee.

Patricia frowned her distaste. "You have to admit, sweetheart, Herman is a dear. I know he's not especially handsome, but he's thoughtful and eager and you could do a lot worse." She raised a perfect eyebrow. "In fact, you have done worse." She shuddered as if remembering some of Mary's previous relationships.

"Yes, Mother, Herman is a dear. But I'll tell you right now, don't start sending out wedding invitations, because I'm not going to marry him."

Exhaustion suddenly weighed Mary down. She was tired of her mother, tired of Herman, and more than anything she was tired of the pressure her mother continually placed on her to hurry up and marry. In Patricia's opinion, if Mary turned thirty and wasn't married, she'd lose any chance at happiness for the rest of her life.

She knew the one sure way to get her mother to cut this visit short. Rubbing her stomach, she grimaced. "Oh, I'm feeling very nauseous again."

As Mary had known she would, her mother jumped up. If there was one thing Patricia Wilshire couldn't handle, it was sickness, especially the spewing kind. "Well, I'd better run along. It's getting late and we're having dinner at the club this evening."

Mary walked with her mom to the front door, where Patricia paused, turning back to her daughter. "Mary, you know I don't mean to be a pain. I just worry about you growing old alone."

Mary leaned forward and kissed her mother's cheek. "I know, Mother."

"Then perhaps you'll reconsider your feelings toward Herman. You've only had one date with him, don't write off a future with him yet. Give him time. Perhaps he'll grown on you," she replied, then hurried down the sidewalk before Mary could once again protest.

Mary shook her head and closed the door. Maybe he'll grow on her...like a fungus or a mold. She sank down on the sofa and thought of her mother's parting words. No matter how tired Mary grew of her mother's meddling and matchmaking, she knew the sole motivation for it was love.

Since Mary's twenty-eighth birthday, her mother had begun a concerted effort to marry her off. And although she found it irritating, she knew the bottom line was that her mother was only worried about her and wanted her to be happy.

Mary's father had passed away four years ago, and after a year of being alone, Patricia had married an old friend. Mary suspected her mother's motivation in marrying Barry hadn't been passion or love, but rather companionship and financial security.

That choice was fine for her mother, but Mary wasn't yet willing to settle for marriage only because she was afraid to live alone. What Patricia didn't understand was that Mary would rather live alone than be with somebody she didn't love with all her heart, all her passion, all her soul. She wanted magic, she wanted the excitement of finding a soul mate, that special somebody who would wrap her up in love and passion forevermore.

Leaning forward, she picked up the thank-you note that had come in the day's mail. A thank-you note from Annie Taylor. Written in bright pink crayon, each letter laboriously correct, the note had touched Mary deeply. Added at the bottom was a thank you from Jonathon, these words written in black ink, the letters bold and masculine.

She ran her fingers over the note, wishing for what could never be, regretting what would never be. There were still times when the fact that she'd never have children hit her like a truck running her down, times when her sadness seemed too deep to bear.

As she stared at the note, she wondered why she tortured herself wishing for something that could never be. Still, that night as she slept, her dreams were filled with Annie's laughter, and Jonathon's evocative eyes.

"What are you going to do about this?" Rachel asked Jonathon. They sat at his table, the latest gift from Annie's mysterious friend before them. It was a basket filled with bubble bath, hair ribbons and watermelon-flavored lollipops.

"What should I do about it? I wrote the woman a thank-you note."

"Doesn't it bother you that this woman sent Annie her favorite kind of lollipops?"

Jonathon shrugged. "So, she made a lucky guess. What's the big deal?"

"The big deal is your lack of curiosity where this woman is concerned." Rachel studied him thoughtfully, curling a strand of her dark hair around her finger.

Jonathon sat up straighter in his chair, having learned long ago that when his older sister started finger-wrapping her hair, he was going to hear something he didn't want to hear. "What's on your mind, Rachel?" he finally asked, knowing he would be sorry.

She smiled and released the trapped lock of hair. "I just don't understand why you're pretending to be wife hunting when you seem to go out of your way to choose dates that are definitely not wife material." She shook her head. "I don't think you want to remarry at all."

"That's ridiculous," Jonathon scoffed. "There's nothing that would make me happier than getting married again and having a complete family. Annie wants a mother and I'd like a wife."

"Then explain the bimbos." Rachel looked at him pointedly.

Jonathon felt heat suffuse his face. "I don't just date bimbos. I went out with Belinda, and she wasn't a bimbo."

"Only because I insisted and set up the date with Belinda," Rachel countered. Again she twisted her hair, her brow wrinkled thoughtfully. "You know what I think?"

"Would it matter if I said I didn't particularly care?" he asked dryly.

Rachel flashed him a bright grin. "No. You know I won't shut up until I've spoken everything that's on my mind."

Jonathon shook his head and laughed. "I know. It's one of your most endearing...and irritating characteristics. So, feel free to continue."

"Why, thank you, don't mind if I do," Rachel smiled, then sobered slightly. "Seriously, Jonathon, I think you deliberately choose women who are inappropriate because you're afraid of loving again."

"That's the most ridiculous drivel I've ever heard," he protested. He grabbed one of the lollipops from the basket, unwrapped it and popped it into his mouth. "If you're going to try your hand at psychoanalysis, you really should get a license." The words were garbled as he spoke around the lollipop.

"No license is necessary for telling my favorite brother hard truths," Rachel countered, letting him know she'd understood every word. She plucked a lollipop from the basket. "I think the reason you haven't shown more curiosity about the mysterious Mary is because you're afraid she'll be a loving, caring woman who just might steal that heart you guard so well."

Jonathon's derisive snort was thwarted by the candy in his mouth. He yanked it out and tried again. "I haven't indulged my curiosity about Mary because I really believe she's probably eighty years old. I don't see the point in expending my energy on finding an old woman who's obviously lonely enough to follow up on a note in a balloon."

"I don't think she's an old woman." Rachel picked up the most recent letter from the lady in question. "Her handwriting looks young, not spidery or shaky. Even the way she's worded the note sounds hip and youthful, and there's the faint scent of perfume clinging to the paper. Definitely not old."

"You think you're so smart," Jonathon said. He leaned back in his chair and eyed his sister with amusement. She'd always been a know-it-all. Unfortunately, most of the time she was right. "I'll tell you what I'll do. I'll find out who this Mary is. I'll even make arrangements to take her out to dinner. But if I find myself in a restaurant with a blue-haired grandmother, then you're going to pay the tab, tip and all."

Rachel laughed. "It's a deal," she agreed. "And now I'd better get out of here. I've still got errands to run before going home."

Jonathon walked with her to the door. "Thanks, sis," he said as she started to leave.

"Thanks for what?" Her eyes twinkled merrily. "For telling you things you don't want to hear?"

"No...thanks for being a good sister."

Rachel kissed him on the cheek. "You're a good man, Jonathon. You deserve some happiness in your life, and you aren't going to find it with one of your bimbos. Find this Mary...at least give it a chance." She started down the sidewalk, then turned back to face him. "And if she is eighty years old and I'm paying for dinner...buy whatever's on special and order the house wine."

Jonathon laughed and waved as she got into her car and drove out of sight.

6

Mary sat at a table in the corner at Antonio's, a popular Italian restaurant, grateful for the intimate lighting that made recognizing other diners difficult.

She couldn't believe she was here, knew she was on a fool's errand, but seemed no longer in control of her own actions.

Three days ago she'd received in her post office box another note from Jonathon Taylor, this one inviting her to meet him for dinner at Antonio's. Although she had no intention of meeting with him or dining with him, she'd come just to see him. Definitely a fool's errand.

She checked her watch. He'd requested her presence at Antonio's at eight o'clock. It was now seven forty-five. Within the next fifteen minutes Jonathon Taylor should walk through the door, expecting to meet the mysterious woman who'd been sending his daughter gifts from her grandmother in heaven.

She was grateful the restaurant was packed, glad her table was situated close enough to the door for her to see incoming diners, yet shoved far enough in the corner that he probably wouldn't notice her.

Toying with the linguini on her plate, she tried to tell herself she was only here because she loved Antonio's clam sauce. However, she couldn't fool herself. She was here for one reason and one reason alone...to see Jonathon Taylor one more time.

It was crazy how often in the past couple of nights he and Annie had invaded her dreams. In the night, when her defenses were down, her fantasies took flight. She dreamed of being in Jonathon's arms, his kisses filling her heart, his caresses evoking shivers of pleasure. She dreamed of his eyes gazing at her with love, with commitment.

Annie also invaded her dreams. Mary dreamed of brushing the child's long golden hair and tucking her in bed at night with kisses and fairy tales. She dreamed of hand-made Mother's Day cards and bouquets of wildflowers, of little girl hugs and mother-daughter secrets.

Morning always brought with it cold reality and a painful hunger in her soul.

As she continued to eat, she kept her gaze focused on the door. Each time it opened to admit new people, her breath caught momentarily in her chest.

She'd just finished the last bite on her plate when he came in.

He flashed a smile at the hostess, a smile that warmed Mary to her toes even though it had not been directed at her. The navy dress slacks he wore hugged his long legs and slender hips, and the pin-striped shirt gave him an elegant though masculine air.

As he followed behind the hostess to a table across the room, Mary watched as women's heads turned in his direction. She'd known that day in the office that he was the type of man who demanded attention. With his dark hair, bold features and gun-metal eyes, he emitted a raw sensuality most women would find appealing.

"Can I get you some dessert?" The waiter's question pulled her attention away from Jonathon.

She didn't really want dessert, but she wasn't ready to leave just yet. "A piece of cheesecake and a cup of coffee," she answered. At least eating the rich dessert would give her a reason to dawdle at the table. When the waiter left, she returned her attention to the man across the room.

He'd ordered a glass of wine, and his focus was intent on the doorway. What did he expect the woman who'd been sending his daughter gifts to look like? A blonde? A redhead? Would he be disappointed when nobody showed up?

What was it about him that so captured her? She tried to analyze why the mere sight of this man caused her heart to race a little bit faster. She had certainly seen men as handsome as Jonathon before, had even dated a few. Still, when she'd looked up from her desk and into his eyes on that day he'd brought Annie into the office, she'd felt a connection, a magnetic pull she'd never felt before.

"Mary. What are you doing here on a Friday night all by yourself?"

Mary jumped in surprise at the sound of a familiar voice. She looked up to see Barbara Watkins, the mother of one of Dr. Burwell's little patients, smiling at her.

"Hi, Barbara. I got hungry for some of Antonio's linguini and clam sauce. How's Kristen doing?"

Barbara's face split into a smile filled with maternal love. "Fine. She's growing like a weed. Can you believe she'll start school this year?"

Mary gasped. "That doesn't seem possible," she protested. "I still remember the first time you brought her in, a squealing little baby with that shock of red hair."

Barbara laughed. "She was probably squealing because of that shock of red hair."

"Is she here with you tonight? It's been ages since you've been into the office."

"No, she's at home with a baby-sitter. Tonight my husband and I are enjoying the company of each other. We're pretending we're on a date instead of just another old married couple." She leaned toward Mary with a wicked grin. "Only my husband knows for sure when he takes me home he's going to score."

Mary laughed, then, saying goodbye, Barbara left to return to her own table. Mary watched her go, envious of the sparkle in her eyes, the flush of color on her face. That's what marriage should be all about, that flush of excitement at the anticipation of making love even after spending so many years together.

Why couldn't she find that for herself? It didn't seem fair that she had so much love in her heart to give, and nobody to give it to.

The waiter brought her coffee and cheesecake and she ate quickly, consciously keeping her eyes averted from Jonathon Taylor. He'd have no trouble at all finding some attractive woman to marry, one who could give Annie lots of brothers and sisters. He and Annie deserved that, a future filled with children and happiness.

She set down her fork, the cheesecake only half eaten. She'd been stupid to come here just to see Jonathon again. Somehow she had to put him and his precious daughter out of her mind. She had to get dreams of him out of her sleep. God, she had to get a life.

Jonathon ordered another glass of wine, wondering where in the hell the mysterious Mary was. He looked at his watch, feeling the frown that wrinkled his forehead. Late. There was nothing he hated more than waiting, and already his "date" was almost twenty minutes late. Not exactly a promising beginning.

She was probably late because her arthritis was acting up, he thought, still convinced the anonymous sender of Annie's gifts was some ancient, lonely old soul. He'd give it another fifteen, twenty minutes, then he'd forget it, go home and eat a bologna sandwich with Annie.

"Jonathon?"

He looked up into a pair of darkly lashed blue eyes. For just a moment he couldn't remember her name, but he had an instant vision of the heart-shaped mole on her inner thigh. Tanya...no, that wasn't it.

Frantically he searched his memory. Trisha...no. Tamara. Bingo. "Tamara, how are you?" He smiled at the buxom redhead he'd dated last year for a couple of months.

She smiled flirtatiously. "I'm doing great." She gestured to a nearby table. "I'm here with a bunch of co-workers, sort of a ladies' night out. What are you doing here all alone?"

Jonathon shrugged, trying to remember why he and Tamara had stopped dating. He looked at his watch once again. "I think I've been stood up."

"Whoever she is, she must be a fool." Tamara sat down in the chair next to him and reached for his glass of wine. With full ruby lips, she took a sip, then set the glass back down. "I've missed you, Jonathon. How's life been treating you since the last time we saw each other?"

"Things have been okay," he began.

"The last couple of months have been horrendous for me." As Tamara catalogued each and every detail of her life for the past eight months, Jonathon suddenly remembered why he had stopped seeing her. Tamara talked incessantly, and only had one topic of conversation . . . herself.

As she droned on and on, he felt his eyes beginning to glaze over, like those of a drunk who'd imbibed too many alcoholic beverages. He sighed in relief as she stood up, saying she needed to get back to her friends. "Call me sometime," she said in parting.

He nodded without commitment, knowing he'd do no such thing. Rubbing irritably at the lipstick smear on his glass, he decided to call it a night. With each moment that passed it grew more obvious that his date wasn't going to show. He'd been stood up.

He paid for his wine, then left the restaurant, a mantle of depression settling around his shoulders. As he drove toward home, his thoughts turned toward his conversation with Rachel. Was she right? Was he making bad choices about the women he dated because deep down in his heart he was afraid?

There was no doubt about it, he'd been hurt by Katherine's abandonment. When he'd spoken his wedding vows, he'd expected years of loving her and building a life together. He'd made a commitment of the heart and had assumed Katherine had made the same.

He could still remember the night Katherine told him she wanted out, that she wasn't having fun anymore. She resented being tied down with caring for Annie, hated that Jonathon, as a commercial pilot, was gone so much.

When she told him she wanted a divorce, he'd actually felt the painful breaking of his heart. His pain had not only been for himself, but also for the little girl Katherine was leaving behind as well.

He'd thought his heart had healed without scars, had believed he'd handled Katherine's desertion in a healthy, positive way. But Rachel's observations suggested otherwise.

Frowning in confusion, he parked in his driveway. He didn't get out, but instead stared thoughtfully at the house he and Katherine had bought together right after Annie's birth. She hadn't lived in it long enough to produce memories. He should be thankful for that.

At the moment he didn't feel very thankful for anything except Annie. Too many disappointments weighed down his heart. He'd hoped to fill the house with the sounds of children's laughter, had always imagined himself with at least two or three kids. He'd hoped the house would one day be overflowing with love.

With every day that passed he was aware of Annie growing older. Soon she would be old enough that having other children would be like having two separate families.

He'd wanted his children to be close together, bonded as he and Rachel were. But he couldn't very well accomplish that unless he found himself a wife.

Unfortunately, he'd realized after his date with Belinda that he wasn't willing to sacrifice and just marry anyone for the sake of more children. He wanted companionship, but more, he wanted the magic that only genuine love could bring. He sighed again, then got out of the car and went into the house.

"Hi, Daddy," Annie greeted him. She and Rachel sat at the coffee table in the living room. "Aunt Rachel and I are playing Go Fish," she explained as she studied the cards in her hand.

"You're home early," Rachel said.

He sank down on the sofa. "She didn't show."

Rachel arched an eyebrow. "Hmm, interesting. I wonder what kept her away?"

"Kept who away?" Annie asked, looking first at her aunt, then at Jonathon.

"My date. She didn't show up," Jonathon explained. He hadn't mentioned to Annie he was going to try to meet her angel on earth, afraid the little girl might be disappointed if she didn't get to go along. Now he was grateful for his decision to keep the information to himself.

Annie placed her cards on the table and crawled up next to him on the sofa. "I'll be your date, Daddy," she exclaimed, and threw her arms around his neck.

He laughed and gave her a hug. "You'll always be my favorite date," he exclaimed.

However, dating and women were the very last thing on Jonathon's mind the next morning. Annie awoke complaining that the porcupine was back in her throat, and by ten o'clock she was once again running a fever.

Thankfully, he remembered Dr. Burwell's office had morning office hours on Saturday. After tucking Annie back into bed, he called the doctor. "Hi, this is Jonathon Taylor," he said to the receptionist. "I was in a couple of weeks ago with my daughter Annie, who had strep throat. I think she's having a relapse and was wondering if the doctor could maybe call in a prescription for some more antibiotics."

"What drugstore do you use?" the pleasant voice at the other end of the line asked.

Jonathon frowned and looked out the window where a chilling rain had been falling since he'd awakened earlier. "You don't know of any drugstores that deliver, do you? I'm not sure I can find somebody to stay with her while I run out, and I really hate to drag her out in this rain."

There was a long pause. "Mr. Taylor, this is Mary. Mary Wellington. I get off at noon. I could get the prescription filled and bring it by."

"I hate for you to go to the trouble," he protested.

"Please, it's not any trouble," she hurriedly assured him. "I often drop off prescriptions for patients. I'll see you between twelve-thirty and one."

"Thanks, I really appreciate it," Jonathon replied. "I'll be waiting for you."

"I'll be waiting for you." For the next two hours those words rang in Mary's ears. As she waited for noon to come, she found herself wondering when exactly she had changed from a healthy, well-adjusted woman to a masochistic person who thrived on self-torture. Offering to take the prescription to the Taylors' house could only be a symptom signaling her descent into some kind of madness.

Still, at 12:17 she stood in the drugstore, waiting for the prescription to be filled. Despite the fact that she told herself over and over again she would just hand Jonathon the medicine, then be on her way once again, she couldn't help the adrenaline that pumped through her at the thought of seeing him once again.

She ran through a driving rain from the drugstore to her car, cursing the foul weather that frizzled her hair and dampened her clothes. Glancing at her reflection in the rearview mirror, she scowled. She looked like a drowned rat.

Why hadn't she worn something different to work today? Why had she yanked on the boring brown slacks and plain white blouse? Why hadn't she worn the red blouse that always brought compliments from her co-workers?

She tightened her hands on the steering wheel. It doesn't matter, she told herself forcefully. I'll just drop off the medicine at the door and get back in my car and drive home. He won't care what I'm wearing. It doesn't matter how I look. All he wants is the medicine for Annie and that's it.

By the time she reached the Taylor house, the rain was a torrential downpour. She remained in her car for a few minutes, but when the rain showed no signs of abating, she grabbed her purse, drew in a deep breath and plunged out of the car. She reached the porch soaked through. Immediately the door flew open and Jonathon pulled her inside.

"Whoa, what a toad strangler," he exclaimed.

"Thank goodness I'm not a toad," she replied.

He laughed and took the small sack that held the prescription from her. "I would have never agreed to you doing this had I known it would be coming down so hard." He frowned. "You definitely need to get out of those wet clothes." His smoke-colored eyes radiated concern.

Mary's heart convulsed in her chest and she fought the impulse to strip naked then and there. Oh, this man had a wondrous effect on her libido. "I'm fine. . . ." She backed toward the door, afraid she'd do something stupid.

"Please." He grabbed her arm, his smile warm and friendly. "The least I can do to thank you is get you dry and offer you a hot cup of coffee before sending you back out into that mess. Come on." He pulled her through the foyer and past the living room, into a bedroom that was obviously his. He disappeared into a connecting bathroom, then reappeared carrying a large navy terry-cloth robe. "You can put this on and I'll throw your wet things into the dryer. While you're changing, I'll give Annie her medicine and make a fresh pot of coffee.''

Before Mary could protest, he left the room, closing the door softly behind him. Aware that water dripped off her and onto the plush carpeting, she ran into the bathroom, the robe clutched to her chest.

Peeling off her slacks and blouse, she looked around the bathroom with interest. Neat and clean, it smelled of men's things, an evocative mixture of shaving cream and cologne. Even the robe smelled of Jonathon. The same spice cologne she'd noticed when he'd been in the doctor's office.

It felt slightly sinful to have his robe against her near nakedness, an intimacy with a man she hardly knew but lusted after. Lust...it had been a very long time since she'd lusted after anyone, but something about Jonathon Taylor had caused a wicked appetite inside her, one she didn't intend to appease.

She left the bathroom and took a moment to stand in his bedroom, stare at the bed where he slept. It was a king-size one, and her mind immediately filled with a picture of Jonathon lounging beneath crisp, cool sheets.

Shoving aside the mental image, she drew in an unsteady breath. She felt like a teenager again, fixated on the high school jock, who'd never given her a second look. Irritated with herself, reminding herself she was no longer a teenager but a woman of nearly thirty, she left the bedroom and wandered out into the living room.

"Mary, in here," Jonathon called from the kitchen. The scent of fresh coffee greeted her as she followed his voice into a cheerful kitchen decorated in reds and yellows. "Here, let me take those." He grabbed her wet things and threw them into a dryer in the utility room just off the kitchen. "Please, sit." He gestured toward the table and Mary slid into a chair.

"I can't thank you enough for getting that prescription for me," he said as he poured them each a cup of coffee, then joined her at the table. "I didn't even want to think about dragging Annie out in this weather, and I couldn't get hold of either my sister or the regular baby-sitter so I could get out."

"Really, I didn't mind," Mary protested. She stared down into her coffee cup, wishing witty and charming conversation would fall from her mouth. Unfortunately, she had a horrible feeling that if she opened her mouth the only thing spontaneous that might come forth was drool.

"So, how long have you worked at the doctor's office?" he asked.

"A couple of years." She looked up into his smiling gray eyes. "What about you? What do you do?"

"I teach classes at the community college."

"Really? What kind of classes?" No matter what he taught, Mary had a feeling he would be one of the most sought-after teachers on campus.

"Airplane engine maintenance and flying. Before I began teaching, I was a commercial pilot for ten years."

"Sounds exciting. I've never been in a plane before."

"Never?" He looked at her incredulously, then shook his head. "I didn't think there were any virgins left." A blush warmed her cheeks and he grinned apologetically. "That's what we call people who have never flown before."

Before Mary had an opportunity to reply, Annie called from a distant part of the house. "Sorry, she probably wants a drink or something," he said as he started to get up.

"Please...could I go to her?" Mary jumped up, one hand clutching the robe closed between her breasts.

He shrugged with an easy smile. "Sure. It's the second door on the right down the hallway."

Mary escaped the kitchen and drew in a deep breath, unable to believe she was in the Taylor home clad in Jonathon's robe. She must be mad. She should have thrust the medicine at him the moment he opened the front door, then turned and run back to her car. She shouldn't have allowed herself to be seduced out of her clothes by the handsome Jonathon Taylor.

Scoffing at her crazy thoughts, she tightened the robe belt around her waist. She hadn't been seduced out of anything. He'd merely done the thoughtful thing in insisting he dry her clothes before she went back home.

She peeked her head into Annie's room, immediately seeing the little girl lying in the bed. Snuggled beneath a fluffy comforter, only her head and shoulders were visible. "Hi, Annie. Remember me?"

Annie frowned for a moment, then brightened. "Mary, from the doctor's office."

Mary nodded and walked into the room, noting the ruffle-bedecked bedspread and pink curtains that gave the room a definite girlish charm. Shelves lined one wall, shelves laden with books, dolls and an abundance of toys. Mary sank down on the bed next to Annie, noting even the little girl's nightgown matched the pink decor of the room. "How are you feeling?"

Annie's lower lip trembled. "I feel terrible," she replied. "My throat hurts and my head hurts and I miss my grandma." She looked at Mary, her eyes misty with tears. "Did you know my grandma is in heaven?" A tear spilled over, running down her cheek. "But I wish she was here with me 'cause I miss her."

"Oh, honey." Without hesitation, Mary gathered Annie in her arms. "I'll bet your grandma wishes she could be here with you, too." Mary stroked Annie's forehead, feeling the heat of fever. Poor little thing, feeling bad and wanting her grandmother. Mary's heart ached with the need to cradle her close, ease the void.

"How come you're wearing my daddy's robe?" Annie asked, not moving from Mary's embrace.

"I brought your medicine to you and it's raining. I got all wet."

Annie smiled, her eyelids drifting closed for a moment. "My daddy says it's duck weather today." Annie looked at Mary again. "Would you keep rubbing my forehead until I go to sleep?" Mary nodded and Annie smiled again. "Good. My grandma used to rub my forehead when I didn't feel good."

Mary continued to stroke Annie's head, realizing that not only was she vulnerable with Jonathon, but with Annie as well. It would be just as easy for her to be seduced by this sweet child as it would be to be seduced by her handsome father.

The minute Annie fell asleep, she needed to grab her clothes and get the hell out of here. She couldn't allow her heart to get entangled with these two people. No matter how she might find them right for her, she couldn't forget how wrong she would be for both of them.

7

—→◆←—

When Mary didn't return to the kitchen, Jonathon went in search of her. He found her in Annie's room, holding his daughter and softly humming a tune he remembered vaguely from his own childhood.

He stood for a moment just outside the doorway, watching the woman and child as his heart did a funny leap in his chest. Strange. When Mary had first appeared on his doorstep, hair bedraggled and soaked to the skin, he'd noticed again that she wasn't the shouting kind of pretty, but rather more of the whisper kind.

However, as she stroked Annie's cheek, a tender smile curved her lips and softened her features, transforming her to the shouting kind. Her hair had dried to form a soft cloud of curls around her face, and without makeup her features shone with a sweet, natural beauty.

A spark of pure, unadulterated desire shot through Jonathon, surprising him. With his robe around her and her hair disarrayed, she looked as if she'd just made love.

At that moment she glanced up and saw him, a smile still curving her lips. He stepped into the room and looked down at his slumbering daughter. "I'm glad you got her to sleep. She had a miserable time last night and didn't get much rest."

Mary eased away from the little girl and tucked her in beneath the pink flowered sheets. "Rest is the best thing for her. The medicine should help her in that regard." She leaned over and touched Annie's forehead a final time, then straightened up and followed Jonathon out of the room and back into the kitchen.

"How about a fresh cup of coffee?" Jonathon asked.

She nodded and smiled shyly, then sat back down at the table. "Annie misses her grandmother," she said as Jonathon poured fresh coffee.

"I know." He rejoined her at the table. "Annie was just three months old when my wife walked out on us. When Katherine walked out, she never looked back. She was killed a couple of years ago in a car accident. My mother was the only mother Annie knew." He swiped a hand through his hair, then shrugged with a touch of embarrassment. "I miss my mother, too."

"I'm sorry," Mary replied softly.

Jonathon looked at her, surprised to see pain in the depths of her eyes, an empathic pain for him. Those lush blue eyes with their soft, shining light rocked him. He broke the gaze...confused, disturbed. "How about some cookies with that coffee?" He jumped up and went to the cabinet and pulled out a package of cookies. "Oreos. Annie's favorite."

"Mine, too." Smiling, she took one from the package. He watched in amusement as she twisted the sandwich cookie apart. She was just about to lick the vanilla filling when she flushed, then laughed. "Okay, I admit it. I always eat them from the inside out."

Jonathon took a cookie from the bag and looked at it thoughtfully. "I've never eaten one that way."

"Ah, I didn't know there were any virgins left." Her eyes sparkled with humor.

Jonathon laughed, amused at her wit and charmed by the blush that accompanied it. "I'll make a deal with you...." He paused and twisted open his cookie. "I'll lose my cookie virginity with you, if you lose your flying virginity with me by allowing me to take you up in my plane sometime."

This time she laughed, a delightful musical sound that seemed to seek and fill the corners of the room. "It's a deal," she agreed, then added, "but I can't believe we're having this conversation."

"Me, neither." He leaned back in his chair and studied her thoughtfully. She was nothing like the women he normally dated. Softer, less colorful... there was a sweet shyness about her he found surprisingly appealing. "So, Mary...tell me what you like to do in your spare time." Knowing his luck she probably enjoyed bottle cap collecting or something equally bizarre.

She shrugged, the robe slipping precariously off one shoulder. She caught it and tugged it back up, but not before he'd gotten a glimpse of creamy satin skin.

Again an arrow of desire stabbed through him, and he realized this woman was a threat like none other he'd dated in a very long time.

"I guess I live a rather boring life. Usually once I get home from the office, I'm too tired to do much of anything. If I have the energy I like taking walks or watching old movies."

He nodded. "I understand that. Between work and taking care of Annie, an evening with the television is sometimes all I can muster energy for."

"It looks like the rain has let up," she said, gazing out the nearby window. "I'm sure my clothes should be dry by now, and I really should be getting home."

Jonathon didn't protest, but instead got up and took her clothes out of the dryer and handed them to her. "You can use my room again to change. Just hang the robe on the back of the bathroom door."

She nodded and disappeared into his bedroom. As he put the coffee cups into the dishwasher, he thought of the conversation he'd had with his sister. Had Rachel been right? Did he go out of his way to date bimbos? Women who could stir his lust but never touch his heart?

Mary Wellington certainly couldn't be classified as a bimbo. He had a feeling she was one of those women who believed in fidelity, commitment, forever. Of course, there had been a time when he'd believed Katherine wanted those same things, and he'd been dead wrong about her.

He slammed the dishwasher closed, irritated with himself and his indecisiveness where Mary was concerned. He liked her smile, found her subtly sexy, so why was he somewhat reluctant to pursue anything further with her? Was it because she wasn't a bimbo? Because she might expect something more from him than healthy lust?

"Thanks for the coffee and for drying my clothes."

He whirled around to see her standing in the kitchen doorway, her lips curved in that shy, sweet smile that did something to his insides. "No problem." He walked with her to the front door. "It was the least I could do for a woman who braved the storm to bring Annie's medicine."

"Me and the mailman. We always deliver our goods." She laughed, and again her musical laughter glided over him like caressing hands. "Well, thanks again," she said, and started out the door.

"Mary?" he called to her as she stepped off the porch. She turned and looked at him, her blue eyes inquisitive. "How do you like pizza?"

"With pepperoni . . . why?"

"I've promised Annie a trip to Uncle Bob's Pizza Palace as soon as she's feeling better. Ever been there?" She shook her head and he continued. "It's an experience you shouldn't miss. We'd love for you to come with us. I'll call you."

She nodded. "Tell Annie I said goodbye, and call the office if she isn't feeling better pretty quickly." With a little wave, she turned and ran for her car.

He watched her drive away, wondering why he'd told her he'd call her. She wasn't his usual type, and he wasn't at all sure he wanted to pursue a relationship with her. Although, she had the nicest eyes, eyes that spoke honesty and openness. And her laughter was warm and melodic. He smiled as he replayed the sound in his mind.

Rachel would probably adore her. Hell, if he introduced the two they'd probably become good friends.

He leaned against the door, his thoughts whirling. If the only reason he was going to go out with Mary was to please Rachel...then why was he so looking forward to a date with her?

"He said he'd call, but it's been almost a week." Mary leaned forward and grabbed another handful of popcorn from the bowl on the coffee table.

"Yesterday you told me you didn't care that he hadn't called, that you were going to turn him down, anyway." Lucinda punched the remote, changing the channel on her television, then looked back at Mary expectantly. "So, which is it? If he calls and asks you out, are you going or not?"

"Why do you care what I do?" Mary asked.

Lucinda grinned. "Because if you intend to turn him down, I thought maybe you could give him my number."

Mary laughed and threw a kernel of popcorn at her friend. "He is attractive, isn't he?"

"Attractive? The man is a heart-stopper, a stud muffin...a hunk who's available and possibly interested in you. If you turn him down, I'm having you committed to the closest mental facility."

Mary pulled her legs up beneath her on Lucinda's sofa, frowning thoughtfully as she stared at her friend. "But isn't it even crazier for me to agree to go out with him, get involved when I know the relationship won't be a long-term one?''

Lucinda punched the mute button, silencing the sitcom on the TV. "Did you know that people who are about to die rarely regret the things they have done, but instead regret the things they didn't do?''

Mary smiled. "So you're telling me to go for it. Don't think about the future, don't think about tomorrow...just have a good time for as long as the ride lasts.''

"That's exactly what I'm saying. Honestly, Mary, even if you're certain you and Jonathon Taylor have no hope for a future, why deny yourself the chance for a wild, wonderful fling?''

A wild, wonderful fling. When Jonathon called two days later to invite her to join them for the next Saturday afternoon at Uncle Bob's Pizza Palace, Lucinda's words fluttered through Mary's mind. Why not? Why not go for the gusto...live for today? Despite her apprehensions, knowing she was a fool to listen to Lucinda, a fool to follow her heart, Mary agreed to the date.

By the time Saturday afternoon came, Mary had changed her mind as many times as she'd changed her clothes. She finally settled on a casual sundress and decided to take Lucinda's advice and have a good time without thoughts of the future.

Once she was dressed, she paced the apartment while she waited for Jonathon and Annie. Cowpoke lounged on the back of the sofa, his enigmatic gaze following her as she walked back and forth before the window.

"Don't worry, Cowpoke, nobody is going to replace you as the only male in my life," she mumbled as she paced. "I'm just going out with Jonathon to have a good time. Nothing serious, no commitment, just for fun."

Cowpoke yawned and Mary scowled. She didn't know why she was talking to the damned cat, anyway. He'd dug three of her plants out of their containers that morning and played with a roll of toilet paper, stringing it all through the apartment. As she'd had with the man who'd owned Cowpoke, Mary had a definite love-hate relationship with the feline.

She turned her attention out the window and saw a dark blue mid-size car pull up and park. Jonathon got out first, then helped Annie from the back seat. Jonathon was clad in a pair of jeans and a short-sleeved T-shirt, and Annie wore a blue shorts outfit. From her distant vantage point, Mary could see the smiles on both their faces as Jonathon took Annie's hand and they walked toward her building.

Her heart fluttered and she moved away from the window, not wanting them to see her peeking out at them. A moment later a knock fell on her door.

"Hi," she greeted them as she opened the door and they stepped into her small apartment.

"Are you all ready for a day of fun at Uncle Bob's?" Jonathon asked.

"We're gonna have fun, Mary. You'll like it." Annie's little body practically vibrated with excitement. "Uncle Bob's has games to play and you can win stuffed animals and little toys and...and..." Annie paused to catch her breath.

"And I guess you're feeling much better," Mary said with a laugh.

Annie nodded. "The porcupine is all gone and I'm tired of staying in bed." Her attention was caught by Cowpoke, who jumped off the back of the couch and approached Annie cautiously. "Oh, pretty kitty."

"Be careful, honey. Cowpoke isn't used to children and he doesn't have a very friendly personality," Mary warned. As if to prove her a liar, the cat curled around Annie's legs, nudging her hand for a petting.

"He looks pretty nice to me," Annie exclaimed, then giggled as Cowpoke arched his back toward her hand.

"He's perverse. If I'd said he was a nice cat, he would have scratched your face just to prove me wrong," Mary observed. She shook her head, watching as the cat continued to court Annie. "I've never seen him take to anyone like that."

Jonathon grinned. "Annie can charm any creature great or small, right, pumpkin?" He looked back at Mary. "Shall we go?"

She nodded, grabbed her purse, and after Annie gave Cowpoke a final farewell kiss on his head, they left.

The midday sun was warm, a hint of the summer months to come. The scent of newly budded flowers rode the warm breeze that blew in through the car windows. As Jonathon drove to Uncle Bob's, Annie kept up a steady stream of conversation, filling Mary in on what to expect from the popular pizza place.

Jonathon kept a bemused smile on his face, obviously entertained with Annie's chatter. As Annie talked, Mary found herself casting surreptitious glances at Jonathon.

She liked the way his hair fell carelessly over his forehead, liked how his eyes crinkled at the corners when he smiled. He had nice hands with long fingers and clean nails. His forearms looked strong and well-shaped with a dusting of dark hair.

Physically, Jonathon Taylor had enough sex appeal to bottle and sell and make a fortune. It would be easy to fall beneath his magnetic, physical appeal. But Mary was smarter than that. Her cowboy had been handsome, with a charming smile that lit up a room, but he'd had the emotional maturity of a ten-year-old. Mary knew that physical attractiveness didn't always mean mental healthiness.

In this case it doesn't matter, she reminded herself. There was no way there would ever be a long-term relationship with Jonathon, no hopes for a future, so she didn't need to worry about how dysfunctional he might be. She intended simply to enjoy this date, have fun and not worry about anything else.

"Looks like a popular place," Mary said as they pulled into the parking lot of the pizza establishment. Most of the parking spaces in the large lot were filled, and it took a minute or two for Jonathon to find an empty spot.

"Every kid in Kansas City has a thing for Uncle Bob's," Jonathon explained as they got out of the car. "And every parent in Kansas City hates the place."

Mary laughed, her heart jumping as he grabbed her hand, then Annie's. "Daddy, you can't hate Uncle Bob's. It's the bestest place in the whole wide world," Annie exclaimed. "You wait and see, Mary. You'll love it, too."

"I knew you'd hate it," Jonathon said moments later as he and Mary sat down in a red plastic booth. Nearby, Annie played with several other kids on a jungle gym.

"I don't exactly hate it," Mary protested. "At the moment I'm simply overwhelmed." Uncle Bob's Pizza Palace was huge. Besides the plastic booths and the ordering counter, arcade games flashed with dizzying lights and crazy noises, and animated figures cavorted across a brightly lit stage.

"It is undeniably overwhelming," he agreed.

"I'm impressed with the hand-stamping," Mary replied, looking at the numbered ink stamp on the back of her hand. Jonathon and Annie had the same set of numbers on their hands.

Jonathon nodded. "We'll be checked at the exit when we leave. That way nobody can walk out with a child that doesn't belong to them. It's the kind of peace-of-mind security that makes parents overlook the chaos and come back again and again."

Mary touched the ink on her hand. "Isn't it sad we have to do things like this to keep our children safe?"

He nodded, his gaze lingering on her thoughtfully. "You must love children . . . I mean with your work with Dr. Burwell and all."

"I do love children," she agreed. Her heart thudded with a dull beat of dread. Tell him. Tell him you can't have children, an internal voice demanded. It's a perfect opening…just tell him and get it out in the open.

"Mary, come and play a game of skee ball with me." Annie appeared at the side of their booth and grabbed Mary's hand.

"How about the three of us play and the loser has to kiss a toad?" Jonathon suggested with a gleam in his eyes.

"But we don't have a toad," Annie protested.

Jonathon grinned. "Ribit."

"Daddy toad," Annie said, giggling as the three of them approached the skee ball machines.

Twenty minutes and three games later Mary was the big loser. "I can't believe you beat me, you little squirt," she teased Annie.

· Annie giggled and clapped her hands in glee. "And now you gotta kiss Daddy toad," she replied.

"Ribit." Jonathon grinned, the gleam in his eyes definitely a wicked one.

As Annie clapped her hands, Mary stood on tiptoes and kissed Jonathon on the cheek. "Darn," she exclaimed as she withdrew her lips from his warm skin.

"What's wrong?" Jonathon asked.

"You were supposed to turn into a prince, and instead you're still a Daddy toad," she teased.

He laughed and placed his hand beneath her elbow to guide her back to the table. "You'll have to give me a better kiss than just a peck on the cheek to transform me from a toad into a prince," he said softly. "Perhaps we can experiment later to see exactly what kind of kiss it takes to make the metamorphosis."

As they slid back into their booth, a flare of wild anticipation swept through her. She had a feeling kissing Jonathon would be a dizzying, bewitching experience.

As Annie continued to play the games and enjoy the various rides the wonderland offered, Jonathon and Mary sat in their booth to await the pizza they'd ordered.

"You have a big family? Sisters or brothers?" Jonathon asked, his gaze going often to his little girl as she ran from game to game.

"No, I'm an only child." Mary smiled ruefully. "Sometimes I wish my mother had more children to worry about, but she only has lucky me to be obsessed with."

Jonathon laughed. "Ah, one of those mothers."

Mary smiled again. "Oh, she's all right. She just worries about me too much. What about you? Brothers or sisters?"

"An older sister, Rachel. She's my best friend and my worst enemy."

"Ah, one of those sisters."

Jonathon laughed. "Definitely one of those sisters." He took a sip of his soda, his gaze lingering on her. "So tell me, Mary Wellington. Why aren't you married and settled down with somebody?"

She shrugged. "I don't know. I guess I'm not very good at the dating game. My mother constantly tells me I have poor taste when it comes to men." She smiled. "In fact, she tells me I'm a jerk magnet."

His laughter caused shivers to dance up her spine. Rich and deep, it stirred something inside her, something warm and pleasant. She knew she could listen to his laughter for a long time and not tire of it.

"My sister claims I tend to draw the wrong kind of women," he observed. "Maybe it's time our luck changed." He smiled, and again Mary's heart fluttered softly.

As the three of them shared pizza, they also shared pieces of themselves. They talked about their favorite colors and preferred foods, and got into a lively argument about whether summer or winter was more fun.

Mary was impressed by how Jonathon encouraged Annie to have her own beliefs. He listened patiently whenever Annie spoke, his gaze soft with love and pride. There was nothing quite so compelling as a loving father, especially one who had broad shoulders, tight jeans and a sexy smile.

It was nearly four o'clock when they left Uncle Bob's. "You in a hurry to get home?" Jonathon asked when they got back in the car.

"Not really. Why?"

"I thought we might buy a loaf of bread and feed some ducks at Annie's favorite pond."

"Oh, yes, Daddy. Let's do that," Annie exclaimed from the back seat.

"Sounds like fun to me," Mary agreed.

It took only a few minutes to collect a loaf of bread, then drive to the city pond where a number of people were out enjoying the gorgeous spring weather.

With Annie armed with the bread, Jonathon reached for Mary's hand, lacing his fingers through hers as they walked slowly along the shoreline.

For several minutes they didn't speak but watched as Annie threw chunks of bread out into the water, drawing the ducks closer to the shore.

Mary looked at the people around them...families sharing a picnic, an older couple sitting in folding chairs with fishing poles extended over the water. She wondered if people looked at the three of them and assumed they were a real family.

With the warmth of Jonathon's hand enfolding hers and Annie's laughter riding on a warm breeze, Mary felt a contentment, a happiness she'd never felt before.

"I started bringing Annie here when she was only a baby," Jonathon said, breaking the comfortable silence. "She was kind of a fussy infant. But the minute I'd put her in a stroller and start walking around the pond, she'd quiet right down."

"She's a lucky little girl to have a father like you."

"No." Jonathon shook his head. "I'm the lucky one to have her. It's amazing how much Annie has taught me about life . . . and love."

Again Mary felt the heady warmth of seduction. This man and his daughter were dangerous. They made her think of things she couldn't have, imagine dreams that could never be.

"I probably should be getting home," she said. It was an attempt to distance herself. She'd been a fool to spend the day with Jonathon and Annie, a fool to tempt herself with forbidden fruit.

He nodded. "Yes, it's getting late and it's been a full day for Annie."

Nearly a half an hour later they pulled into Mary's apartment complex. Annie slept in the back seat, her face smudged with dirt and a slice of bread still clasped in her hand.

"Tell Annie I said thank you for introducing me to Uncle Bob's and for sharing her favorite pond with me," Mary said as she opened the car door and stepped out.

"I'll tell her," he agreed as he slid out of the car and joined her. Together they walked toward the front door of Mary's apartment. "And thank you for a terrific day," he added. "I'm glad you shared the day with us."

Mary unlocked the door and reached for the knob, but paused as Jonathon stopped her with a hand on her arm. "Wait a minute, you can't go in yet," he protested, the wicked, sexy gleam in his eyes. "You promised me you'd try to break the curse that has kept me a warty toad all these long years."

"I don't remember making any such promise," she replied, her heartbeat unsteady as he leaned closer to her. His scent surrounded her, the pleasant spice smell beckoning her closer.

"Oh, I distinctly remember," he murmured, then moved his mouth to cover hers.

Hot and hungry, his lips claimed hers with fiery intent. She wanted to hold back, not respond, but the physical sensations overwhelmed the mental rationality, and with a small groan, she wound her arms around him.

He deepened the kiss with his tongue as his hands pressed against her back, pulling her intimately against the firm planes and hard angles of his body.

Mary succumbed willingly, molding herself to him with abandon. It was crazy, it was madness pure and simple. And it was the madness she clung to, not wanting to think, not willing to reason.

When the kiss finally ended, Jonathon expelled a deep breath. "Whew, I think I passed the prince stage and have gone straight to king." With his index finger he traced slowly down her jawline, his eyes filled with warmth... desire.

With effort, she stepped back from him. "Good night, Jonathon," she said, then with a small wave, she went inside.

Once there she leaned weakly against the door, waiting for her heart to stop its frantic pounding. Sweaty palms, racing heart, shortness of breath, all the symptoms were there. She was definitely on the verge of falling in love once again.

Squeezing her eyes tightly closed, she willed back the tears that threatened to fall. Jonathon wasn't a toad, but he wasn't a prince or a king, either. He was simply another Mr. Wrong and she was a stupid fool.

8

━━━━◆◆━━━━

As Jonathon drove home, he tried to forget the woman he'd just spent the day with, tried to ignore how her laughter had warmed him and her kiss had shocked him.

He drew in a deep breath as he thought of that kiss. Definitely, sweet Mary had surprised him with the depth of her response, the utter lack of artifice and total emotion and heart in her kiss.

Heart. That's what frightened him. He had a feeling Mary Wellington had more heart than all the women he'd dated in the past five years put together. She intrigued him. She tantalized him. Something about her scared the hell out of him.

After tucking Annie into bed later that night, he stood in the doorway of her room, watching her as she slept. He wanted to give his daughter her dreams of a mommy and brothers and sisters, but he knew in order to do that he'd have to make himself vulnerable again.

If he was smart, he'd make a marriage of convenience. He'd find a pleasant, attractive woman to marry and bear his children without the emotion of love to complicate things. However, the idea of living his life with somebody he didn't really love was repugnant. And the idea of opening his heart and risking heartache was frightening.

For the first time he acknowledged to himself that Rachel might be right, that the scars Katherine had left were deep. Maybe he should listen to his big sister more often.

Was he ready to risk his heart again? He didn't know. Only time would tell ... time and perhaps the right woman. Definitely he intended to see Mary again. Time would tell if she was his Ms. Right.

As he went into the living room, he realized there was something else he wanted to follow up on ... the mysterious Mary who continued to send Annie gifts. The latest, a stack of picture books, rested on top of the coffee table, along with the note that had accompanied them.

He wondered if Rachel was right about Mystery Mary as well? Was it possible she wasn't a blue-haired old woman with dozens of cats, and was instead a loving, caring young woman who'd been touched by Annie's initial balloon note? Odd that two women named Mary had made such an impression on him in such a short time.

The phone rang and he grabbed the receiver, at the same time sinking down into the sofa. "So, how'd it go?" Rachel asked. He'd told her earlier that morning that he was spending the day with Dr. Burwell's receptionist.

"Good. We had a nice day."

"So when are you taking her out again?"

"I don't know. I thought maybe I'd ask her to go to the zoo next weekend with me and Annie."

"Sounds good, but when are you going to have a real date with her?"

Jonathon frowned. "What do you mean, a real date?"

"I mean just you and this woman without Annie as a buffer."

For a moment Jonathon was silent, his brain working over his sister's words. Did he use Annie as a buffer? Certainly her presence made dates easier for the most part. He sighed, hating it when Rachel was so smart, so rational. "I don't know, I don't want to rush things."

"You'd better think about rushing things, little brother. You're thirty-five years old. You're lucky you still have all your hair, but who knows what might happen in the next year or two. You'd better find your life partner before you go bald or get a pot belly."

"Good grief, Rachel, was this call meant to make me paranoid?" Jonathon asked as he snaked a hand through his hair to assure himself it was still thick and full. "Besides, you're one to talk. It's been six years since your divorce from Harry. When are you going to find a nice man and settle down?"

"Ah, clever. When uncomfortable with the conversation, turn it around." Rachel laughed. "Nice try, little brother, but we're talking about you, not me."

"But we could talk about you," he countered.

Rachel sighed. "The difference between us is that I like being alone. I'm satisfied not being married. You aren't. I don't mean to be a pain, I'm just giving you a reality check. Jonathon, you've been single for a long time. I've heard it gets more and more difficult to make a relationship work after you've been alone for so long."

Jonathon sighed. "Rachel, ease up, would you? It's enough that Annie is pressuring me to get married and plant baby brother and sister seeds."

Rachel laughed. "I've been meaning to talk to you about that. The other day when Annie was over here she told me if you didn't hurry up and plant seeds, then she'd just have to do it herself. She's going to plant seeds in the backyard and see if she can grow a baby in the garden."

Jonathon groaned, knowing another talk about babies and birth was in order for Annie. He frowned as another thought entered his mind. "Rachel, promise me that if I don't ever remarry that you'll be the one to take Annie for her first bra and you'll have the talk with her about becoming a woman."

Again Rachel laughed. "It's a deal, but surely you'll be happily married long before Annie needs a bra."

"Who knows what fate has in store for me."

"Jonathon, you are the master of your own fate. Ms. Right isn't going to just walk into your life. You're going to have to work to find her . . . and speaking of that, have you found out any more about your mystery gift giver?"

"No, although first thing Monday morning I plan to go to the post office where her box is located and see what I can find out. I have to admit, something about her gifts and her attention to Annie is starting to bother me. I want to know who she is."

"Who knows . . . maybe she's Ms. Right," Rachel said hopefully.

"We'll see," Jonathon replied, although he had a feeling he'd already met a possible Ms. Right in Mary Wellington. But he'd only know for sure after a little more time and a few more dates.

For some reason, he was reluctant to forge ahead with Mary Wellington until he'd met the Mystery

Mary who had become such a large part of Annie's life.

After all, Rachel could be right. Perhaps the Mystery Mary would be the woman who'd make his dreams come true.

Monday morning Jonathon walked into the small post office where the mystery woman's box was located.

Funny, this particular post office station wasn't far from Mary's apartment building. He toyed with the idea of stopping by for a quick cup of coffee, then remembered she'd be at work at the doctor's office.

Approaching the counter, he pulled a piece of paper out of his pocket where he'd written the post office box number. "Excuse me, could you tell me the name of the woman who rents box number 12241?"

The gray-haired man shook his head. "Sorry, we can't give out that information."

"But I just need her last name," Jonathon protested. "Can't you give me that? I know her first name is Mary."

Again the clerk shook his head. "No can do. I could lose my job for giving you that information."

Jonathon could tell there was no way he could cajole the man to give him what he wanted. He turned away from the counter in frustration. What now? How on earth could he meet this woman if she refused to meet him and hid behind the anonymity of a post office box?

And why the need for such secrecy? What was she hiding? Why not meet him and get to know Annie on a more personal basis? Walking back out to his car, he continued to question the Mystery Mary's motives. Why hadn't she met him for dinner the night they'd arranged an encounter?

He sat in the car and stared at the post office. His only alternative was to haunt this place until he saw the woman getting mail out of box 12241. He frowned, knowing that wasn't a viable alternative. He didn't have the time it would take to hang out here until he managed to stumble onto his mystery woman.

From the post office he headed toward the college, where his first class would begin in thirty minutes. Maybe he should just concentrate on work and being the best daddy Annie could ever have. Perhaps it was time to tell Annie there might not be any little brothers or sisters, and there might not be a new mommy.

He frowned as he imagined Annie's little face, her bottom lip quivering in disappointment. No, he couldn't shatter her dreams just because his own had been shattered so long ago.

Somehow he had to trust in love again, for Annie . . . but more important, for himself.

* * *

"Magic," Mary told her mother. "I'm not seeing Herman anymore because there was no magic between us."

"Oh, honestly, Mary. You're far too old to be waiting around for magic." Patricia dabbed at her mouth with her napkin, then placed it back on her lap. "Magic is for schoolgirls, not grown women."

Mary didn't answer, but instead stared down at her salad. She wanted to tell her mother about Jonathon... about magic, for that's exactly what she felt when she was with him and Annie. Their date to Uncle Bob's had been followed up with an afternoon at the zoo and a trip to an Italian restaurant where Annie had entertained them by showing them how to eat spaghetti without using utensils.

However, she couldn't tell her mother about the magic of Jonathon and Annie. There was no point. Mary knew it was only a matter of time before the magic would go "poof" and disappear in a puff of smoke.

Patricia signaled the waiter for more coffee and Mary mentally groaned, knowing her mother would continue the lectures as long as the coffee was strong and fresh.

She should have never agreed to this lunch. Jonathon and Annie were coming to dinner that night and she should be home cleaning her apartment, preparing the special meal.

"Honestly, I just don't understand you," Patricia continued as the waiter filled her cup, then departed. "You never were a fanciful child. I raised you to be a rational young woman, and rational women don't wait around for magic."

"I know, I know, especially when they're almost thirty and will never have children," Mary replied wearily.

"Now, Mary, I didn't say anything when you were dating that dreadful cowboy, but it breaks my heart when I see you turning your back on a perfectly nice man like Herman."

Mary shoved her plate away and stood up. "Mother, if you love Herman so much, divorce Barry and marry Herman." She tossed her napkin on the table. "Just make sure before you do, you cut that dreadful hair between his eyes." Before her mother could reply, Mary said a terse goodbye and left the restaurant.

Once out on the sidewalk, she drew in a deep breath, knowing before the day was over she'd need to call her mother and apologize for her rudeness. Still, she was sick of her mother singing the praises of a forty-five-year-old man who still asked his mother for permission to date. Herman was a nice man, but he wasn't the man for her.

And neither is Jonathon, she reminded herself an hour later as she polished her living room furniture. During the couple of dates she'd spent with Jonathon and Annie, one theme had remained. Annie wanted sisters and brothers. The subject was rarely far from her mind. Jonathon was a wonderful father, and should have a houseful of children, something Mary would never, ever be able to give him.

Still, she hadn't told him that, hadn't mentioned that she couldn't have kids. The opportunity simply hadn't presented itself, and besides, she wasn't ready to stop the relationship yet, and she knew telling him about her inability to have children would end it all. She couldn't blame him. He and Annie had dreams... dreams she couldn't help fulfill.

Heaven help her, but she wasn't ready to stop seeing Jonathon and Annie. Their presence filled an emptiness in her life. Magic.

At six o'clock the house sparkled, the scent of chicken cordon bleu filled the air, and Mary had changed from her sweats into a pair of navy slacks and a light blue flowered blouse.

"You be nice to Annie tonight," she told Cowpoke as she put on a touch of makeup. The cat lounged in the center of the bed, like an arrogant king on a velvet throne.

"If you aren't nice to her I'll make you eat that cheap cat food instead of the gourmet stuff you love," she warned. Her heart skipped a beat as her doorbell rang. With a final glance in the mirror, she turned and ran to let them in.

"Hi," she said, looking in surprise at Jonathon, who stood alone outside her door. "Where's Annie?"

"I left her with her Aunt Rachel," he said as he stepped inside. "I thought it was time we two adults had some quality time."

"Oh." Mary's heart stepped up a beat at the warmth his gaze contained as he looked at her.

"You aren't disappointed, are you?"

She shook her head. "Of course not...I mean, I adore spending time with Annie, but quality time with you is nice, too." She felt the blush that swept over her face as his grin widened.

He touched the tip of her nose with his finger. "You have the cutest blushes," he said as he moved past her and into the living room.

Sinking down on the sofa, he gestured for her to join him. "Come and tell me about your week."

"Let me just check on dinner. How about a glass of wine?"

"Sounds great. Can I help?"

"No, I'll be right back." She escaped into the kitchen where she turned down the temperature on the oven, then retrieved the bottle of wine from the refrigerator. She paused a moment before returning to the living room, needing to get her nerves under control.

On all the dates they had shared thus far, Annie had been with them, a buffer, an insurance that the relationship wouldn't transcend to a physical level.

But tonight there was no Annie. Only Jonathon, looking devastating in a pair of worn jeans and a short-sleeved gray sports shirt. Jonathon, who'd walked in and filled the living room with his overt masculinity and dangerous sex appeal.

Maybe tonight she'd find the opening to tell him she couldn't have children. Dread coursed through her at the thought. She knew how the scene would play out, had lived it too many times in the past not to know. She would tell him she couldn't have children. He would pause, make some inane comment and his eyes would darken with a tinge of pity. It wouldn't take long before he would make up some excuse to call it a night, and she would never hear from him again. Maybe she wouldn't even look for an opening tonight. She wanted the magic to continue just a little while longer.

"Here we are," she said as she reentered the living room with the wine and glasses. She sank down next to him on the sofa.

"Let me," he offered, taking the wine bottle from her. His fingers lingered on hers as he handed her a glass of white wine. "Now, tell me about your week," he said, his gaze so warm on her she wondered if she might suffer internal combustion.

"There's a flu bug going around. Jason Weekly threw up in the waiting room. Lucinda has a new boyfriend, and my mother is still driving me crazy." She waved her hand dismissively. "But you don't want to hear about all that."

"I do," he protested. "I like knowing what's going on in your life when I'm not with you." He reached out and took her hand in his. "Now, let's take it one at a time. Is Jason Weekly feeling better?"

Mary laughed, trying to ignore the shivers that begged to shimmy up her spine as his thumb rubbed little circles of heat on the back of her hand. "Yes, it's just a twenty-four-hour bug."

"And what about your friend Lucinda? I thought she was dating some guy she met at Sebastian's?"

"She was, but that fell apart and she's now dating one of the medical supply salesmen who come into the office. I don't know if she'll ever settle down. Unlike me, she likes the dating game."

"The dating game." Jonathon winced. "Personally, I think whoever invented dating should be drawn and quartered."

"Yes, but what's the alternative? No dating, no relationships? I'm afraid the pain of the dating game is inevitable." She wished he'd stop caressing her hand. His gentle touch made it difficult for her to think, impossible to concentrate on casual conversation, impossible to concentrate on anything but the warmth and sensuality of his touch.

"The last two weeks I've found very little painful about the dating game," Jonathon said, his gaze caressing her as potently as his fingers.

"Tell me about your week," she said, then sipped a bit of the wine. His heated gaze made her mouth dry, her palms damp.

"Nothing exciting in my week except for trying to get a name from your local post office clerk."

She frowned. "What do you mean?"

"Somebody has been sending Annie gifts in the mail and I've been trying to find out who it is." As he went on to explain about the balloon and the mystery woman, Mary kept her features carefully schooled, asking questions anybody would ask. She'd just about decided to tell him she was the benevolent gift sender when he changed the subject and began talking about his classes.

Still his hand held hers, his thumb moving in sensual little circles and evoking a flame of heat inside her. When he fell silent for a moment she broke the physical contact and stood up. "I'd better get dinner on the table. I'm sure you must be hungry."

"Starving." Although, the glint in his eyes made her think his answer had nothing to do with food.

Again an internal heat swirled through her as she went back into the kitchen.

"You mind if I put on a little music?" Jonathon called from the living room.

"Not at all, help yourself." It took only a few minutes to get the salad out of the refrigerator, take the chicken out of the oven and slice up a crispy loaf of bakery bread. She'd just put the final touches to the table when the sound of soft, romantic music filled the apartment.

She looked up and saw him leaning against the doorway, a seductive smile curving his sensual lips. "Come dance with me, Mary." He walked across the room and took her by the hand.

"But dinner..."

"Can wait," he finished, pulling her into the living room and into his arms.

"It's been years since I've slow-danced with anyone," he murmured in her ear. "I've always found slow-dancing one of the most intimate forms of communication."

Certainly slow-dancing with Jonathon was the most intimate activity Mary had indulged in for a very long time. His long legs and strong thighs pressed against hers, leading her with strength and grace as they moved across the floor.

His hands moved up and down her back. Slowly. Sensually. Igniting flames of heat each place they touched. Mary leaned her head against him, a hand splayed against his chest, where his heart thundered as loudly as her own.

She closed her eyes, falling into the magic of being in his arms, enjoying his masculine strength as they swayed to the sounds of her compact disk player.

Her breath caught in her chest as he dipped his head and kissed her neck. Hot. His lips burned with a pleasant heat as they trailed down the length of her neck, then back up to capture her earlobe.

Mary leaned into him, her knees weakened by the desire that shot through her. She tried to stifle a low moan as his hands splayed over her buttocks, pulling her closer, more intimately against him.

She knew she should call a halt, stop the dancing, the seduction, before she fell completely beneath his spell. *People only regret what they don't experience.* Lucinda's words replayed in her mind and she cast prudence to the wind, allowing her desire to overtake her.

"Mary."

She looked up at him and he captured her lips with his in a hungry kiss that swept away any remnant of caution she might have entertained. He deepened the kiss, his tongue exploring as his hands moved up beneath her blouse, caressing the bare skin of her back.

Mary knew they were going to make love. The promise of it was in his kiss, in each languid stroke of his hands. She wanted it. For one night in her life she wanted to make love with a man who gave her magic. She would face the consequences in the light of day, but tonight she wanted Jonathon holding her, kissing her, loving her.

As their kiss lingered, all pretense of dancing ceased. Instead, their bodies melded together and moved to the rhythm of desire.

When the kiss finally ended, Jonathon gazed at her, his gray eyes deeper, darker than she'd ever seen them. And in their depths, she saw a question and knew he was giving her the option of continuing or stopping.

She stepped away from him and took his hand. With wild anticipation sweeping through her, she led him to her bedroom. Once there she released his hand and began to unbutton her blouse.

Twilight had fallen outside, casting the room in shadows and dusky illumination, but the golden slivers of light streaming in the window only added to the dreamlike quality in Mary's mind.

She had unfastened half her blouse buttons when Jonathon gently pushed her hands away and took over the task. As he worked her buttons, she unfastened his, wanting to see his chest, feel the warmth of his skin beneath his shirt.

The moan she'd stifled earlier escaped as he slid her blouse off her shoulders and his lips touched the hollow of her throat, then trailed across her collarbone.

He paused only long enough to remove his shirt and take off his slacks, leaving him clad in a pair of white cotton briefs that left little to her imagination. He sat down on the edge of the bed, then pulled her to stand directly in front of him.

With his lips pressed against her stomach, his fingers worked the snap and zipper of her slacks, then he slipped the material down her hips and to the floor. Wrapping his arms around her waist, he eased them both down on the bed.

"You are beautiful," he murmured.

"So are you," she whispered, awed by the perfection of his broad shoulders, slender hips and flat abdomen. His chest was firm, covered with springy hair that coiled around her fingers as she caressed him.

Another moan escaped her as he unfastened her bra and pulled it off, exposing her to his heated gaze. His hands covered her breasts as his mouth once again sought hers.

Within minutes they were both naked, exploring the mysteries of each other. Despite the newness and the wild anticipation Mary felt and knew Jonathon shared, she was pleased he seemed to be in no hurry.

Instead, he took his time, as if he intended to enjoy the foreplay for as long as possible.

Mary was grateful he wasn't a verbal lover, but seemed to prefer to communicate by his gaze, his hands and his mouth. Her cowboy had had a penchant for shouting "yahoo" at critical moments, effectively breaking the spell with the lusty cry.

Jonathan was perfect...a dream lover with hands of fire and lips of flame. Magic. It sparkled in the air, snapped in an arc between them, exploded in her heart. When finally he entered her, the emotion and the rightness of the moment brought tears to her eyes.

He moved against her, then stiffened, a bellow erupting from him. The sound reverberated in the room, dispelling the magic she'd felt only moments before. She froze, wondering if every man in the world made loud, obnoxious noises in the throes of passion.

"Eoowww," he cried again, scooting away from her and grabbing for his back. Mary sat up, wondering if this was part of some strange sex ritual. Just her luck, Mr. Right had a weird fetish.

Her dismay fell away as she realized why he was yelling. Claws firmly implanted into his skin, Cowpoke rode his back, hissing and spitting as Jonathon tried to get him off.

Mary jumped up and grabbed the cat, wincing as she finally managed to dislodge him from Jonathon. She put Cowpoke out of the bedroom and then closed the door. "I'm so sorry," she exclaimed. "He's never done anything quite like that before."

She walked over to where Jonathon stood by the side of the bed and looked at his back, where thankfully the skin had just barely been broken. "He's had all his shots, but maybe you'd better let me clean you up with some rubbing alcohol."

He turned around to face her, amusement curving his lips. "You sure know how to show a guy an exciting time," he observed.

Mary giggled, pleased he wasn't angry at the unusual interruption. "Come on." She took his arm, intending to take him into the bathroom to clean him up.

"Am I bleeding much?" he asked.

She turned him around and looked at the wounds Cowpoke had inflicted. "Not really," she replied.

"Then forget the clean-up," he said, taking her in his arms. "Now, where were we?"

As he pulled her back on the bed, the magic returned.

9

Much later Jonathon and Mary sat at the kitchen table, feasting on cold chicken cordon bleu, slightly stale bread and wilted lettuce salad. It was the best meal Jonathon could remember eating for a very long time.

In fact, he felt better than he had in a long time, and knew his euphoric feeling was due to the company. Even in silence, he felt in tune with her, as if important communication was taking place without the need for words.

As they ate, he gazed at her, enjoying how her tousled hair framed her face, the flush of color on her cheeks and the sparkle in her eyes. She looked beautiful. Thoroughly sated and contented.

Making love to Mary had made him realize how empty his lovemaking had been before her. Before Mary he'd just been going through the actions, accepting pleasant physical sensations without involving his heart and soul. But with Mary it had been different, and he knew he was falling in love with her.

He could easily imagine them sharing coffee in the mornings, a couple of kids at the table creating the loving pandemonium of family. She'd make a good mother. He'd seen her enough with Annie to know her heart was filled with love. More important, she would make a good wife. She was the first woman he'd dated whom he thought he could wake up to each morning, hold in his arms every night.

"You're staring," she said, breaking the silence that had grown between them.

"Yes, I am." He grinned at her. "You look very pretty."

She blushed. "I've heard cat scratches can cause dementia. I think you're exhibiting the first stages."

He laughed. "And I think we should spend quality time together more often."

The color on her cheeks deepened and she focused back on her plate. Jonathon found her shy blushes charming, knew that beneath the shyness was passion. He'd tasted her passion, experienced her abandon. Yes, this was a woman he could spend a lifetime loving.

He'd spent enough time with her to know she wasn't another Katherine. Mary had the spark and charm of Katherine without the selfishness and irreverence for all he held dear.

Careful, guy, he cautioned himself. *Don't move too fast. You've only had a handful of dates with her. Give it more time. Be very sure this time.* But despite the brevity of their relationship, he was sure.

For the remainder of dinner they small-talked, the easy, silly talk between two lovers. Never had Jonathon felt so at ease, so comfortable with a woman. He didn't feel the need to try hard to be entertaining like he had with so many of his previous dates.

When they finished the meal, he helped her with the dishes, then realized it was getting late and he should leave. As Mary walked him to the door, regret swept through him. Regret that he couldn't spend the night and wake up in the morning with her in his arms. Regret that they couldn't make love one more time before the night was over.

At the doorway, he took her into his arms, needing to taste her lips one final time before leaving. "It was a wonderful meal," he said.

She smiled up at him. "It would have been better had we eaten first."

"I think it was perfect just the way it was."

"It was," she agreed, her eyes deepening in hue. "And I'll know next time you ask me to dance with you that you have something else in mind."

He laughed. "And I hope you slow-dance with me again very soon." He dipped his head and kissed her, reveling in the sweetness of her lips. He broke the kiss and lingered at the door. "I'll call you tomorrow," he finally said. She nodded, and with a little wave, he left.

Mary closed the door after him. She walked to the sofa and sank down, heart heavy. She'd known it was a mistake to make love with Jonathon, known it and had done it, anyway. And it had been wonderful, irresistible... magical.

Her body still tingled with the memory of his hands, his lips, his body moving against hers in perfect synchronization. He'd been a dream lover, full of passion and tenderness, giving pleasure as well as taking.

Covering her face with her hands, Mary played and replayed the evening and the times they'd shared together in the past several weeks. She'd taken Lucinda's advice. She'd gone for the gusto. Every minute she'd spent with Jonathon and Annie had been a joy, and at no time had Mary guarded her heart. They'd gone to the zoo, shared several meals, and in all the time she'd shared with them, Mary had embraced them both wholeheartedly, with no thought or worry about the future.

Now, the future was here. She couldn't fool herself or pretend any longer. Yes, she'd gone for the gusto, lived for the moment and now she had to face the consequences of her actions. And the consequence was that she had fallen desperately, hopelessly in love with Jonathon.

"Fool," she said aloud to herself, her vision blurring as tears filled her eyes. She'd known from the very beginning that Annie and Jonathon could never be for her. She'd known from the beginning that they wanted a woman who could give Annie a brother or sister, give Jonathon a second child. She should never have gone out with them to begin with, should never have involved herself in their lives.

Now she was stuck with the consequences and didn't know what to do. It wasn't fair to Jonathon to continue seeing him, wasn't fair to pretend there was any kind of a future for them. He and Annie still had dreams, but hers had shattered the day the doctor performed her hysterectomy. It wasn't fair for her to pretend she could in any way be a part of their dreams.

Before the tears could completely overwhelm her, she went to bed, seeking solace in dreams. When she awakened the next morning she felt no better. Sunday stretched before her, empty and lonely. Jonathon said he'd call, but she didn't intend to answer the phone. There would be no more contact with Jonathon.

She'd send one last gift to Annie, then she'd break that contact as well. Sooner or later if she kept sending things, she'd make a mistake, give away a clue that would lead to Jonathon figuring out her identity. Better if he never knew. With the precision of a surgeon, she had to make the final cut clean and final.

She'd just finished dressing and had poured herself a cup of coffee when the telephone rang. Carrying her mug into the living room she sat down on the sofa next to her answering machine. The machine picked up after the third ring. Herman's voice filled the room. He'd called several times over the course of the past two weeks, but Mary hadn't returned any of his calls, figuring that if he didn't hear from her he'd get the message she wasn't interested.

As she listened to his message, requesting her company for dinner that evening, she thought of her mother's words. She'd found her magic, but what good had it done her? Maybe her mother was right, the best reason to marry was for companionship and security. Herman could give her both...and he didn't want children.

She grabbed up the phone. "Herman, I'm here."

"Mary, I've been trying to get in touch with you for the last couple of weeks."

"I've been in and out a lot," she answered, trying to ignore the ache of her heart. "But I'm here now and I'd love to have dinner with you this evening."

She closed her eyes as Herman expelled his enthusiasm. After making the necessary arrangements, they said goodbye. Mary hung up the receiver, her gaze captured by the crystal angel sitting next to the phone.

She picked it up, the glass figurine cool and smooth in her hands. Her grandmother had bought the piece for Mary's eighth birthday, and it would make a perfect final gift to Annie. Somehow, Mary thought her grandmother would approve.

Her grandmother would approve and Annie would love the gift. And her mother would be happy she was having dinner with Herman. Yes, everyone was happy... everyone except her.

Jonathon enjoyed Sundays. Lazy days that began with Annie bringing him the paper in bed. While he read, she'd cuddle next to him and watch cartoons on the bedroom television. It was at these times that Jonathon and his daughter shared their most important conversations.

He finished reading the sports pages, then set the paper down, waiting for a commercial to break into the cartoon action. He didn't have long to wait. "Annie, come here and give your old dad a hug," he said.

"Okay, but you're not old," she said, hugging him around the neck then kissing him on the cheek.

"Can I talk to you for a minute?"

She sat back up and nodded. "What do you want to talk about?"

"I was wondering what you thought of Mary?"

"Mary from the doctor's office?" Jonathon nodded. "I like her," Annie replied. "She made me feel better when I was sick, and she's lots of fun." Annie frowned. "But she's kind of stinky at skee ball."

Jonathon laughed. "She just needs more practice." He hesitated a moment, then continued more seriously. "Do you think she'd make a good mommy for you?"

Annie nodded her head vigorously. "Are you gonna marry her and plant some seeds, Daddy?"

"Would you like it if I married Mary?"

Annie giggled. "Marry Mary. Marry Mary." She said the words like a cheerleader leading a chant, then frowned thoughtfully. "Daddy, how long does it take to grow a brother or sister?"

"Almost a year," Jonathon answered.

"A year?" Annie's frown deepened. "I'll be old by the time you make me a brother or sister. Maybe we should just get a pony instead."

"A pony?" Jonathon laughed, surprised at this new request. "But where would we keep one?"

"If it was little enough, it could stay in my room with me."

Jonathon laughed again. "I'm sorry, pumpkin. I think a pony is out of the question." He gave her a quick kiss on the cheek. "But I'm going to see what I can do about getting you that new mommy and perhaps a little brother or sister as well."

Throughout the morning and afternoon, Jonathon argued with himself. It was too soon for him to feel this way about Mary, and yet he couldn't ignore what his heart told him. Despite the fact that they'd only had a handful of dates, in spite of the fact that they'd made love only once, it was enough for him to know she was the woman he wanted to spend the rest of his life with, the woman he wanted to share his dreams with.

How did she feel about him? Surely she'd felt the same kind of magic he'd experienced when they'd made love. Surely she'd felt the very rightness of being in each other's arms. Her eyes had spoken love to him, her touch had communicated the same emotion. Crazy? Perhaps. The only thing he knew was that Mary Wellington had touched him where nobody else had managed to since Katherine. She'd given him hope, she'd renewed old dreams, she'd made him want to try again to recapture the magic of love.

By the time he got a moment alone to call her, it was early evening. Annie was in the bathtub after a day spent at the park, giving Jonathon a few minutes to himself. He first called Rachel and invited her to dinner the next evening.

"What's the occasion?" Rachel asked.

"I want you to meet Mary."

"The mystery woman?"

"No, not that Mary," Jonathon explained. "Rachel, obviously the Mystery Mary doesn't want to be found and I can't think of any way to find her. The Mary I want you to meet tomorrow night is the woman who works at the doctor's office." He paused a moment. "She happens to be the woman I intend to marry."

There was a long pause. "Is this some kind of a joke?"

Jonathon laughed. "I swear, no joke."

"When you picked up Annie last night why didn't you say something?"

Jonathon leaned back against the sofa, remembering the emotions that had filled him up so completely when he'd left Mary's apartment the night before. "I don't know, it was all too new...too strong to share last night."

"Oh, Jonathon, I'm so happy for you. So, tell me all about her."

"I'm not sure what to say...she's pretty, she has a wonderful sense of humor." His mind flashed with moments shared with Mary. "She has a sweet blush and she loves Oreo cookies. There's no one single thing that really stands out, except that I've fallen in love with her."

"That makes her pretty special. What time tomorrow?"

Jonathon frowned. "I don't know, I haven't spoken to Mary yet. I think she gets off work around five. Why don't we make dinner about six-thirty?"

"Sounds perfect...what can I bring?"

"A bottle of bubbly. I'm hoping we'll be celebrating my engagement."

"You got it."

As soon as Jonathon hung up with his sister, he dialed Mary's number. After three rings her answering machine picked up. Jonathon fought down a surge of disappointment. "Mary, it's me, Jonathon." He frowned, words of love on the tip of his tongue, but somehow it didn't seem right to spill them to a machine. "Mary...just wanted you to know you've been on my mind. How about coming over here for dinner tomorrow night? I've invited my sister. About six-thirty. If you can't make it, call me."

He paused a moment, then grimaced as the beep sounded, indicating the end of his message time. As he hung up, he remembered all the symptoms that went along with falling in love. He felt both hot and cold, scared she loved him and terrified she didn't. Oh, God, he'd forgotten how miserable being in love could be.

* * *

Mary was just about to walk out her door when she heard Jonathon's voice on her recorder. She fought the impulse to snatch up the receiver and instead grabbed her purse and left the apartment to meet Herman, who'd pulled up in the parking lot.

"Gosh, Mary. You look great," he enthused as she joined him at the curb.

"Thanks." She was wearing the red dress her mother liked and had pulled her hair up in a French knot that threatened to gift her with a killer headache before the night was through.

She slid into the passenger seat and forced a smile at Herman as he got in and started the engine.

"I made reservations at The Green House for dinner," he said. "I hope that's all right?"

"Fine. I've never eaten there before, but I've heard it's a wonderful restaurant." She settled back in the seat, trying to ignore the distracting hair that sprouted between his eyes. Was it possible it had grown longer in the past two weeks? Did it work like a compass, always pointing north? She bit her bottom lip, stifling a hysterical giggle.

Companionship. Security. She reminded herself of all the things that were important. Magic couldn't sustain itself beneath the harshness of reality. No amount of magic could make her right for Jonathon.

Maybe Herman will grow on me, she thought, listening absently as he spoke about a patient's painful bunions. At least if she married Herman she'd never have to worry about foot problems.

The Green House restaurant was a popular, although expensive, eating establishment. Inside, lush exotic plants and natural-looking waterfalls provided an attractive backdrop to the candle-lit tables carefully placed for maximum privacy.

"I must confess, I thought perhaps you were avoiding me when I couldn't get in touch with you the past couple of weeks," Herman said once they were seated and had placed their dinner order.

"It's just been a busy couple of weeks," she hedged. Oh yes, I've been busy, she thought. I met a man, fell in love, shared a single night of passion, then made a date with you.

Herman nodded, as if with perfect understanding. "I think it's important that a woman have her own interests, her own career, don't you?"

"Absolutely," she agreed, trying to ignore the irritating, dull pounding at the base of her skull. Wearing her hair up always gave her a headache. She took a sip of her wine and forced her attention back to her date.

"I know in my first marriage part of the problem was that my wife had nothing except me and the children to focus on. I kept telling her to get a part-time job or volunteer some hours of the day to a lo-cal charity, but she didn't listen to me.''

I would have been happy focusing on children, Mary thought with an uncharacteristic surge of self-pity. It wasn't fair that she loved children, yet had been denied the pleasure of having them. She took another sip of her wine, the dull pounding at the back of her head increasing in intensity.

She breathed a grateful sigh as the waiter ap-peared with their orders. Perhaps eating would help alleviate her headache.

As they ate, once again Mary found her attention drifting from the man she was with to another man. Jonathon. He filled her thoughts with pleasure and pain. When had she fallen in love with him? Had it been that first time she'd seen him, when she'd looked up from her desk and into his soft gray eyes? Or had it been later, on one of the afternoons they'd shared? A million moments were captured in her brain, like snapshots securing special memories for-ever. Jonathon's laughter, so deep and rich. His pa-tience and enormous love for his daughter was only one element of his character that made her love him. So many memories, ones that filled her with a bit-tersweet longing for what might have been.

Then there was Annie, sweet little Annie. As easy as Jonathon had been to love, Annie had been easier. Bright and funny, she was full of affection and had willingly shared her affection with Mary.

"Mary?"

She flushed and looked at Herman. "I'm sorry, my mind took a momentary vacation."

He nodded. "Speaking of vacations, I have a medical convention to go to next week in Pittsburgh. Would you be interested in tagging along with me?" Before she could answer he hurriedly continued. "Separate rooms, of course. Although I'll be in meetings most of the day, each night we could paint the town red."

Paint Pittsburgh red? "I don't think I could get the time off work," she replied. "But thank you for asking me."

"Maybe another time," he replied, his gaze warm as he continued to look at her. "I like your hair that way. It looks very chic."

He pronounced it *chick* and once again Mary bit down on her bottom lip to prevent an outburst of hysterical laughter. "Thank you," she managed to murmur.

Relief coursed through her when they finished eating and Herman indicated he needed an early night. "I've got surgery early in the morning," he explained as they walked back to his car. "A bad case of ingrown toenails."

"Sounds painful," Mary replied.

Herman nodded. "People don't realize how the health of their feet reflects on their entire body. Sore, tired feet make a sore, tired person." He smiled at her. "Sometime I'll give you one of my super-duper foot massages and you'll see it makes you feel like a whole new person."

Would it take away her heartbreak? Would a good foot massage ease the pain that racked her each time she thought of Jonathon and what might have been? Somehow she didn't think so.

"Thank you, Herman. Dinner was lovely," she said once they had arrived back at her apartment and stood at her front door.

"It was nice, wasn't it?" he agreed, then leaned forward and gave her a soft kiss on the cheek. "Good night, Mary. I'll call you some time this week."

"Good night, Herman." Mary went into her apartment, wishing Herman's sweet kiss had made her blood sizzle, caused a shudder of sudden desire to sweep through her. But there was nothing. No magic.

As she walked into the living room the blinking light of her answering machine captured her gaze. One message. Jonathon's. Sinking down on the sofa, she stared at the spasmodic red light. Love. Love. Love. It seemed to taunt her, tempt her.

Watching it blink, she realized one thing. She couldn't keep Herman dangling. She would never marry him and it wasn't fair of her to keep dating him, giving him the hope that a long-term relationship would result.

She reached up and pulled the pins from her hair, allowing it to tumble around her shoulders, but her headache didn't ease. Standing up, she punched the delete button on her answering machine. She went into her bedroom and changed into her pajamas.

Cowpoke protested with a mewl as she moved him off her pillow so she could get into bed. "Oh, be quiet," she muttered irritably. Tears filled her eyes as the cat curled up against her side.

This was far worse than any case of unrequited love. Jonathon liked her, perhaps even loved her. And she loved him. Like Romeo and Juliet or Antony and Cleopatra, a love destined for doom.

Even if she were foolish enough to continue dating Jonathon, eventually he'd realize the sacrifice was too great. He was a virile man who deserved children of his own, a family to carry his name through generations. He'd find another woman, one who could make him and Annie a bigger family.

She'd rather experience the heartache now than years from now if they married and Jonathon looked at her with regret and disappointment.

10

> ◄━━━━

"Maybe she didn't get your message," Rachel offered as she and Jonathon cleaned up the dinner dishes. They'd waited until after seven to eat, assuming that Mary would arrive any time, but she'd never shown up.

"Maybe," he replied. He scraped the last of the roast beef down the garbage disposal, fighting against a wave of depression. It was crazy, but now that he'd realized the depths of his feelings for Mary, he couldn't wait to tell her.

He wanted to explain to her how long he'd waited for her to come along, how she'd made him believe in happily-ever-after at a time when he'd lost all faith in that particular concept. He needed to tell her he loved her, that he wanted to spend the rest of his life loving her.

"I'll call her tomorrow and see what happened," he said as Rachel handed him the last of the dirty dishes from the table.

"I'm sure it's nothing to worry about. Either she didn't get your message or went out of town or something," Rachel suggested as she gave his shoulder a reassuring squeeze.

Jonathon placed the remaining dishes in the dishwasher, then started the machine. As it hummed to life, he and Rachel carried coffee into the living room.

"Have you done anything more to find out the identity of the other Mary?" Rachel asked as she sank down on the sofa.

Jonathon shook his head. "I don't know what else to do. Besides, my number one priority is to go ahead with my life with Mary. I want her as my wife, and I want to give Annie the brothers and sisters she's been bugging me about for the last six months." He sat down next to her and placed his mug on the coffee table. "I want a family. A real family, and I want it with Mary."

Rachel smiled. "She must be some woman."

"She is." Jonathon settled back against the sofa cushions, knowing a lovesick smile curved his lips. "When I first saw her, I really couldn't imagine myself getting serious about her. Now I can't imagine living my life without her."

"Definitely sounds like love."

He nodded, then frowned. "The crazy part is I want to tell her I love her right now. I don't want to wait another minute. It took so long to find her I don't want to waste another minute without her.''

"Then what are you doing sitting here?" Rachel asked, her brows raised in amusement.

"What?"

"If you don't want to wait another minute? If you're bursting to tell this woman you love her, what are you doing sitting on your duff with me?" She smiled. "Go...get out of here. I'll baby-sit Annie and you go spill your guts to the woman you love."

Jonathon didn't wait for his sister to make the offer twice. He jumped up, grabbed his car keys and headed for the door. Once there he paused and looked back at Rachel. "You're a good big sister, Rach," he said.

She grinned. "I know. I'm the best."

Jonathon laughed, then left the house and got into his car. As he drove toward Mary's apartment, doubts ripped through him. Was it possible he'd misread her?

No, he knew women could fake pleasure during lovemaking, but there was no way he'd believe that Mary had faked anything. Love had radiated from her eyes as they'd eaten their late-night meal. Love had been in her kiss when he'd told her goodbye.

Looking back now on the dates they'd shared, he realized he'd felt her love before they'd actually made love. It had been in the touch of her fingers when she spoke to him, in her body language when they'd been together. No, he hadn't been wrong. She cared deeply for him, as he did for her, and it was right that he take the relationship to the next logical step.

He stepped down on the gas pedal, eager now to start his lifetime of happiness with Mary. Even exceeding the speed limit, it took him twenty minutes to reach Mary's apartment complex.

After parking the car, he gazed up at the second-floor apartment, glad to see a light on, hoping that meant she was home. He took the stairs two at a time, his heart pounding with apprehension and anticipation.

When he reached her door, he knocked briskly. Come on, Mary. Be home. He realized his heart thundered louder than his knock. Nerves. He couldn't remember ever being so nervous, or ever feeling like he had so much at stake.

Come on, Mary. He knocked again. Maybe she was in the shower, or on the phone. He waited a few minutes then knocked loudly one last time. Still no answer.

Disappointment surged inside him as he lingered for another long moment, then stepped back from her door. Apparently she wasn't home. His proclamation of love, his marriage proposal, would have to wait.

He took the stairs more slowly going down, wondering if Mary might be out of town. Perhaps her mother lived out of town. In their brief conversations about her mother he'd never asked if the woman lived in Kansas City. Or maybe she'd gone on some kind of a business trip? Surely if she'd gotten his message about dinner that night she would have been at his house. Surely she wouldn't just blow him off.

As he got in his car, he looked back up at what he knew was her living room window. A silhouette appeared for just a split second, then disappeared. He frowned, his stomach muscles clenching as he continued to stare up at the window in confusion. She was home. She was home and she hadn't answered his knock.

And if she was home, surely she'd gotten his message about dinner. Why hadn't she come? Why hadn't she answered the door?

He started his engine, the answer to his questions rolling around in his head. He felt sick to his stomach, ill with stupidity. She hadn't come to dinner because she didn't care about him. She hadn't answered his knock because she was avoiding him. She didn't love him. She'd just effectively blown him off.

Over the next couple of days, Jonathon tried not to think of Mary, but no matter how he tried, she invaded his thoughts, continued to fill his heart.

In the middle of his classes, he would suddenly forget his lecture, his brain instead filled with visions of Mary. He thought of the sweet blushes he'd found so endearing, her melodic laughter that always made him respond in kind.

Late at night, when Annie was asleep, he wandered his house, consumed with thoughts of Mary. Even when they had only sat together sharing the events of their days, there had been something magical about it. Inane conversation had seemed stimulating with Mary. Life had become exciting with her in his life.

Even his dreams were filled with her. Erotic dreams replaying their lovemaking haunted him. The feel of her skin was imprinted on his fingertips, the taste of her lips made thoughts of kissing anyone else abhorrent.

It had been relatively easy falling out of love with Katherine. When she abandoned him and Annie, the abandonment had left scars, but the callous way she'd walked out on them had made it easier for the love to fall away.

He didn't know how to fall out of love with Mary. Even though he felt she'd somehow used him, misled him, even though he wanted to forget her, he simply didn't know how.

On Wednesday evening, he sat on the sofa, staring at the television, not watching but instead thinking of Mary. What he couldn't understand was how he could have been so wrong. Something special had clicked between them. Magic. How was it possible she hadn't felt it when it had been so strong in him?

"Daddy?"

Annie's voice broke his reverie. "Yes?"

She walked over to where he sat and climbed up next to him. "Are you sad?"

He smiled at her, as always amazed at the perception of children. "A little," he admitted.

Annie wiggled closer to him and wrapped her hand around his thumb. "Is it 'cause Mary isn't going to marry us?"

"Yes, I guess that's part of it." Yes, he was mourning the fact that obviously Mary wasn't destined to be in his life. More, he was grieving his loss of dreams once again. It had taken him so long to get past the wall he'd erected around his heart. He'd finally succeeded at that, only to be hurt once again. He looked down at his daughter. "I was hoping for a wife for me and a new mommy for you."

Her little fingers tightened around Jonathon's thumb. "Daddy, a new mommy would have been nice, but I'm awful glad I got you as my daddy."

Jonathon couldn't speak for a moment. His heart was too full. If he lived a million lifetimes, he'd never understand how he got so lucky to have a daughter like Annie. He pulled her into his lap and hugged her tight.

Mary was the loser here. He and Annie had so much love to offer. They were half a family just waiting for the right woman to make them complete. However, Jonathon knew even if they never found that special woman to be his wife and Annie's mother, he and Annie would be all right alone.

"Daddy, I didn't show you what I got today in the mail." Annie scrambled off his lap and disappeared into her room. She reappeared a moment later, a crystal figurine held in her hand.

Jonathon took the delicate angel from her, a frown tugging at his brow. "You got this from the Mystery Mary today?"

Annie nodded. "And she sent me a letter to tell me she won't be writing to me anymore."

"Where's the letter?"

"In my room. Want me to get it?" As Jonathon nodded, Annie disappeared once again. She returned a moment later with a piece of stationery. Jonathon scanned the note, surprised to find it did indeed say that this would be the last gift to Annie. The note said that Annie's grandma had assigned the Mystery Mary to another job because she knew Annie was going to be just fine.

"Isn't it pretty?" Annie said, taking the angel back from him. "I love it. It's just like the one Mary has in her apartment."

"What?" He looked at Annie in surprise.

"Mary has one just like it. I saw it when we went to pick her up when we went to Uncle Bob's," Annie explained.

Coincidence? Jonathon wasn't sure. The post office box that belonged to the Mystery Mary was very near Mary's apartment building. He stared at the letter in his hand, then remembered the appointment card Mary had written out for him when he'd taken Annie to the doctor.

As Annie returned to her bedroom to play, Jonathon went to his room in search of the appointment card. He checked the top of his dresser where he often emptied his pockets at the end of the day. No card. In the closet, he methodically checked pockets, exclaiming in triumph as he pulled the card out of the pocket of a pair of slacks.

Returning to the living room, he placed the card next to the letter on the coffee table. The writing appeared to be the same. Why hadn't he realized it before? It was the only thing that made sense. Two Marys in the same part of town, both involved in his life. He'd been blind not to realize it before.

Mary had rejected him and now appeared to be rejecting his child. Anger suddenly gripped him. It was one thing to play head games with a man, quite another to play them with a child.

Within minutes he'd arranged for Rachel to watch Annie and he was in the car heading for Mary's place. He wasn't sure what he intended to say to her, he knew only that he needed to confirm that she was, indeed, the Mystery Mary. Beyond that, he had a feeling what he needed most from her were answers. Had she felt the magic... or not?

Mary checked the table one last time, trying not to remember that the last time she'd had a male over for dinner they had made love. Tonight it would certainly be different. Tonight over a home-cooked meal she would tell Herman there was no hope for them to have a continuing relationship.

The scent of stuffed pork chops filled the air. The salad was chilling in the refrigerator and a plate of spiced apple rings adorned the table next to a basket of warm rolls.

As she stirred the corn warming on the stovetop, she tried not to think of Jonathon. How difficult it had been remaining silent when he'd knocked on her door Monday night. She'd wanted to fling the door open and fly into his arms. She'd wanted to taste his passion one last time, but she knew she'd be the worst kind of fool to do so. She'd already been foolish enough for a lifetime.

The doorbell rang and she looked at her watch. Seven-thirty. Herman was always punctual. Opening her door, she forced a smile as she greeted Herman. "Come in," she said.

He shook his head. "Uh, Mary, something has happened." His gaze skittered away from her and down to his feet. "I...uh...I can't have dinner with you tonight...."

"Herman, what's wrong?"

He looked at her, a sheepish smile on his face. "Nothing is wrong. Everything is right." He took one of her hands. "Mary, you're a lovely woman and I'm sure someday you'll find the right man for you."

Mary stared at him in surprise. This was beginning to sound like a dump. "Herman, what's happened?"

"What's happened?" A beatific smile stretched his lips. "Mary, it sounds crazy, but last night Mother invited over a woman for me to meet. I went to appease Mother. I certainly didn't expect anything, but the moment I saw Wendy, something happened. It was wild...it was crazy...it was...it was..."

"Magic." Mary smiled, truly happy for Herman.

"Yes. Magic," he agreed. "I know I should have called earlier, but the day zoomed by and I didn't get a chance."

"Don't worry about it," Mary replied. She squeezed Herman's hand with affection. "I'm happy for you, Herman. I hope you and Wendy have a wonderful life together."

He leaned over and kissed her on the cheek. "I knew you'd be a good sport. You're a special person, Mary. I hope you find a little magic of your own."

As Herman bounded back down the stairs, Mary closed her apartment door, fighting down a burst of laughter. She'd set a beautiful dinner to prepare the stage for letting Herman down gently, and instead he had found his own brand of magic with somebody else.

She frowned as somebody knocked on her door once again. Had Herman forgotten something? "Herman?" She pulled open the door and froze, her eyes locking with angry gray ones.

"Who's Herman? A new conquest?" Jonathon swept past her into the living room. "Are you going to break his heart, too?"

Mary closed the door, her heart thudding as he turned to face her. His features were taut with anger, his mouth a thin slash. Oh, God, even in his fury he was gorgeous, and she steeled herself against the impulse to stroke the anger away from his brow, kiss the strain from his sensual lips. "What do you want, Jonathon?" she asked.

"Look, I don't care what kind of games you play with me, but I won't have you playing games with Annie."

She stared at him in surprise. "What are you talking about?"

"This." He pulled the familiar crystal angel from his pocket.

Mary felt the warm flush that rose to her face as she stared at the gift she'd sent Annie. He knew. "Okay, I confess. I'm the mystery woman sending things to Annie."

Her confession seemed to momentarily stun him. He stared at her for a long moment, his eyes losing some of their storminess and instead radiating confusion. "Why, Mary?"

She shrugged. "I found Annie's balloon blowing across the parking lot at the doctor's office. I read her note and it touched me. Initially I had no thought of getting involved in your life. I just figured I'd send a couple of gifts, a few letters and help a little girl get over her grief. Then you asked me out and things got more complicated."

"Things got complicated?" He laughed, a short, bitter sound. Again he gazed at her, searching her features as if for answers to a question she didn't understand. "Mary? What happened? I thought we were building something special here. Why have you been avoiding me?"

Because I love you. Because I don't want to hurt you and Annie. So many answers swept through Mary's head, answers she didn't feel she could say to him. Tears of frustration burned her eyes and she merely shrugged.

He walked over to her and placed his hands on her shoulders. "Mary? Talk to me. I need to know if I'm the fool here. Did I just imagine how special things were between us? Did I want it so badly I fooled myself?" Genuine pain radiated in his voice. "For God's sake, I'm in love with you, and I thought you felt the same way."

Mary moved out of his grasp and turned her back on him, unable to face his pain as tears spilled onto her cheeks. "Jonathon, I'm not the right woman for you, so what difference does it make how I feel?"

"What do you mean you aren't the right woman for me?" Once again his hands took her shoulders and he twirled her back around to face him. "Talk to me, Mary. Surely I deserve at least that much."

Once again Mary shrugged his hands off her shoulders. "This is all crazy," she exclaimed, angry with fate, tormented by the reality of her own inadequacies. "It's all my fault, I should never have gone out with you to begin with. I knew it was just fate laughing in my face, but I couldn't help myself."

"What are you talking about?"

"I'm not the woman for you. I can't be your wife or Annie's mother. It's crazy for us to continue seeing each other because I'm all wrong for both of you."

"What's wrong with you?" Jonathon matched her tone, his voice raised to the same near-shouting level as hers.

"I can't have children." The words exploded out of her, followed by a gulping sob. "I can't give Annie brothers or sisters. I can't build a family with you."

Air whooshed out of Jonathon and he sank down on the sofa. Mary's heart felt like a stone in her chest. Surely now he understood, and at least their relationship would have a proper closure. "It's not something that can be fixed. I had to have a hysterectomy several years ago." She closed her eyes, for a moment unable to look at him. She didn't want to see him as his confusion changed to unhappiness, as his love changed to pity. As tears burned at her eyes, she swallowed hard against them, unwilling to let him see her cry. Drawing in a deep, steadying breath, she looked at him once again. "And now you see that there's no place for our relationship to go," she said softly. "I can't fulfill your dreams. I can't give you what both you and Annie want. It's silly for us to continue seeing each other."

He raked a hand through his hair and stared at her, his mouth once again set in a grim line. He took the angel figurine out of his pocket once again and set it on her coffee table. For a long moment he looked at the angel, his brow furrowed as a muscle ticked in his jaw. "How audacious it is of you to decide what my dreams should be."

"What?" Mary looked at him in surprise.

His gaze met hers, once again stormy gray with anger. "What right do you have to make decisions for me? Decide what dreams I should seek and which ones aren't important?"

"But Annie..."

"Is a child," Jonathon replied. "And she's already decided if she can't have a brother or a sister she wants a pony." He stood up and approached where Mary stood. "What Annie needs more than anything is a mother who will love her and make her feel safe and secure. What Annie needs most to be healthy and well-adjusted is to know her daddy loves her mommy and they live together in love.

"Mary, if all I wanted was a woman to bear my children, I'd have married one of the women I've dated before. But they didn't touch me the way you have. I didn't love them the way I love you."

Again tears filled Mary's eyes as she heard the words she'd so longed to hear spoken by the man she loved with all her heart. "Oh, Jonathon, I love you, too. But I'm so afraid."

"Afraid of what? I want you to marry me, be my wife, be Annie's mother. We're a family, and we don't need other children to make us happy. If sometime in the future we decide we want more children, we'll adopt. There are all kinds of kids out there who need loving parents."

"But I wouldn't be able to stand it if someday you looked at me and regretted being married to somebody who can't give you your own children."

"Mary..." He breathed her name softly, sweetly, at the same time pulling her into his arms. "The only thing I could ever regret was if I let the perfect woman for me walk out of my life. You and Annie are all I need to make my dreams come true. Marry me. Be my wife. Be Annie's mother."

"Yes," she whispered. This time the tears that fell from her eyes were tears of happiness. "Oh, yes, Jonathon." As he moved his lips to hers, she tasted the promise of a lifetime of love, of sharing dreams, of building a future.

When the kiss ended, she remained in his arms, looking into his beautiful gray eyes. "The first time I saw you, something happened to my heart. And the first time we kissed, I knew I was in deep trouble. It was crazy... it was awesome... it was... it was..."

"Magic," he replied.

"Yes. Magic." As his lips sought hers again, she felt the magic winging its way through her body, searing itself into her soul. It was magic, all right, the magic of love.

Epilogue

―――►◄―――

"Annie, get Angel out of the flower bed," Jonathon said as he raked at the colorful autumn leaves that decorated the back yard.

Mary stood at the back door, watching her husband, her daughter and the new puppy that had brought havoc to their lives. Angel, a mongrel of undetermined lineage, was a ball of black fur and a bundle of curiosity and energy.

"Daddy, she likes flowers," Annie exclaimed, giggling as the dog nuzzled through the impatiens, then paused to give Annie a lavish lick on her cheek. "She likes flowers and me." Annie spied Mary at the back door and waved. "Mommy, come and watch Angel. She's eating Daddy's flowers."

Mommy. Even after a year, Mary still thrilled at the sound of the word, a title she'd never thought she'd hear directed at her. She stepped out on the back porch. "Annie, you have to teach her not to eat the flowers." Mary picked up a tennis ball from the porch and tossed it toward Annie. "Get her to play ball with you."

"Come on, Angel. Get the ball." As Annie coaxed the dog, Mary walked over to Jonathon, who had stopped his work and now leaned against the rake, a warm smile curving his lips as he gazed at her.

"I hope that dog wasn't a mistake," he said.

"How can you even think she was a mistake? Look at that." She pointed to the dog, now climbing onto Annie's lap, licking her face while Annie's giggles rode the autumn breeze. "She adores that dog. Besides, surely it will be easier to train than a pony."

He laughed and put an arm around her shoulder. "Happy?"

She smiled at him. "You know I am." Mary had never known the happiness she'd had since marrying Jonathon. Mary's mother had never been so happy as when Mary married Jonathon. Mary smiled at this thought. "I invited Mother and Barry for dinner tomorrow night."

"What are you fixing?"

"Chicken cordon bleu."

A wicked gleam lit his eyes and he tightened his arm around her shoulder. "Hmm, that reminds me of something. . . ."

"Stop!" She laughed, knowing he was talking about the first time they'd made love, then had eaten cold chicken cordon bleu afterward. She jumped as the phone rang. "I'll be right back." She ran for the back door and disappeared inside.

Jonathon watched her go, contentment surging inside him. He'd never known happiness until this past year with Mary. She filled up his life more than he'd ever dreamed possible. He wondered sometimes if his mother hadn't somehow guided the path of that red balloon, taking it to the one woman who was meant for him.

"Jonathon."

He turned at the sound of Mary's voice. She ran toward him, her face glowing as laughter bubbled from her. "What is it?"

"On the phone. It was Serena Johnston." She looked at him expectantly.

His heart stepped up its rhythm. Serena Johnston worked at the adoption agency. "What did she say?"

Mary jumped up and down. "She has a baby for us. A little boy, three weeks old. She's waiting for us to come and pick up our son."

Jonathon stared at her, stunned by the news they'd waited so long to hear. Immediately after their marriage, Mary had begun checking into the adoption process, insisting she wanted a brother or sister for

Annie. Jonathon merely wanted whatever made Mary happy. But now, happiness exploded inside him. A boy. A son for him and Mary to raise along with Annie.

Mary laughed and threw her arms around his neck. "Oh, Jonathon, we have a son." Tears of joy sparkled in her eyes as she released him and turned toward Annie. "Sweetie, put Angel inside. We have to leave and pick something up."

"Why? What are we gonna get?" Annie asked. She put the dog in the house, then turned back to her father and mother.

Jonathon walked over to her and scooped her up in his arms. "We're going to go get you a baby brother."

"Really?" Annie's eyes widened in wonder. "A brother?"

With Annie riding on his hip, Jonathon placed an arm around Mary and together they headed for the car.

"But, Daddy, you didn't even tell me you planted seeds," Annie protested as Jonathon backed the car out of the driveway.

"Sometimes you can get a baby brother other ways," Jonathon said, searching for a way to make Annie understand. "Sometimes dreams come true and you get what you wish for and it's like...uh..." He looked at Mary for help.

She smiled, the soft, glowing smile of a woman loved. "It's magic, Annie. Sometimes it's just sheer magic."

Jonathon grabbed Mary's hand across the seat. Yes, magic...with a little help from one red balloon.

* * * * *

Morgan Brigham slowly set down his coffee cup on the kitchen table and stared at the comic strip in the center of his paper. It was nestled in among approximately twenty others that were spread out across two pages. But this was the only one he made a point of reading faithfully each morning at breakfast.

This was the only one that mirrored *her* life.

He read each panel twice, as if he couldn't trust his own eyes. But he could. It was there, in black and white.

Morgan folded the paper slowly, thoughtfully, his mind not on his task. So Traci was getting engaged.

The realization gnawed at the lining of his stomach. He hadn't a clue as to why.

He had even less of a clue why he did what he did next.

Abandoning his coffee, now cool, and the newspaper, and ignoring the fact that this was going to make him late for the office, Morgan went to get a sheet of stationery from the den.

He didn't have much time.

Traci Richardson stared at the last frame she had just drawn. Debating, she glanced at the creature sprawled out on the kitchen floor.

"What do you think, Jeremiah? Too blunt?"

The dog, part bloodhound, part mutt, idly looked up from his rawhide bone at the sound of his name. Jeremiah gave her a look she felt free to interpret as ambivalent.

"Fine help you are. What if Daniel actually reads this and puts two and two together?"

Not that there was all that much chance that the man who had proposed to her, the very prosperous and busy Dr. Daniel Thane, would actually see the comic strip she drew for a living. Not unless the strip was taped to a bicuspid he was examining. Lately Daniel had gotten so busy he'd stopped reading anything but the morning headlines of the *Times*.

Still, you never knew. "I don't want to hurt his feelings," Traci continued, using Jeremiah as a sounding board. "It's just that Traci is overwhelmed by Donald's proposal and, see, she thinks the ring is going to swallow her up." To prove her point, Traci held up the drawing for the dog to view.

This time, he didn't even bother to lift his head.

Traci stared moodily at the small velvet box on the kitchen counter. It had sat there since Daniel had asked her to marry him last Sunday. Even if Daniel never read her comic strip, he was going to suspect something eventually. The very fact that she hadn't grabbed the ring from his hand and slid it onto her finger should have told him that she had doubts about their union.

Traci sighed. Daniel was a catch by any definition. So what was her problem? She kept waiting to be struck by that sunny ray of happiness. Daniel said he wanted to take care of her, to fulfill her every wish. And he was even willing to let her think about it before she gave him her answer.

Traci sighed. Daniel was a catch by any definition. So what was her problem? She kept waiting to be struck by that sunny ray of happiness. Daniel said he wanted to take care of her, to fulfill her every wish. And he was even willing to let her think about it before she gave him her answer.

Guilt nibbled at her. She should be dancing up and down, not wavering like a weather vane in a gale.

Pronouncing the strip completed, she scribbled her signature in the corner of the last frame and then sighed. Another week's work put to bed. She glanced at the pile of mail on the counter. She'd been bringing it in steadily from the mailbox since Monday, but the stack had gotten no farther than her kitchen. Sorting letters seemed the least heinous of all the annoying chores that faced her.

Traci paused as she noted a long envelope. Morgan Brigham. Why would Morgan be writing to her?

Curious, she tore open the envelope and quickly scanned the short note inside.

Dear Traci,
I'm putting the summerhouse up for sale. Thought you might want to come up and see it one more time before it goes up on the block. Or make a bid for it yourself. If memory serves, you once said you wanted to buy it. Either way, let me know. My number's on the card.

Take care,
Morgan

P.S. Got a kick out of *Traci on the Spot* this week.

Long, lazy afternoons that felt as if they would never end.

Morgan.

She looked at the far wall in the family room. There was a large framed photograph of her and Morgan standing before the summerhouse. Traci and Morgan. Morgan and Traci. Back then, it seemed their lives had been permanently intertwined. A bittersweet feeling of loss passed over her.

Traci quickly pulled the telephone over to her on the counter and tapped out the number on the keypad.

* * * * *

*Look for TRACI ON THE SPOT
by Marie Ferrarella, coming to
Silhouette YOURS TRULY
in March 1997.*

They were only together

For the Baby's Sake

Or were they?

Look for this heartwarming collection about three couples getting together for the sake of the children— and finding out along the way that it isn't only the children's needs they're fulfilling...

Three complete stories by some of your favorite authors.

BROOMSTICK COWBOY
by Kathleen Eagle

ADDED DELIGHT
by Mary Lynn Baxter

FAMILY MATTERS
by Marie Ferrarella

Available this February wherever
Harlequin and Silhouette books are sold.

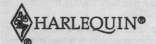